MASSES OF ASSES

Teachers and Taught in Scottish Schools since World War II

James Fyfe

Copyright 1997

James Fyfe

ISBN 1 872350 42 9

Published and typeset by
GC Book Publishers Ltd.,
North Main Street,
Wigtown,
Scotland. DG8 9HL
email: sales@gcbooks.demon.co.uk
www.gcbooks.demon.co.uk

Printed and bound in Great Britain by
MPG Books Ltd, Bodmin, Cornwall

FOREWORD

I think it is true, or true enough, to state that one of the subjects most frequently and regularly discussed in the press and on television is education, which would suggest that much is wrong with the system; anything that works well is never allotted such coverage.

Since the end of the Second World War secondary education in particular has undergone radical changes in almost every conceivable aspect. This book is an attempt to present a critical picture, but sometimes in not too serious a vein (perhaps something of a paradox when dealing with such a serious matter) of how the Scottish system has developed or misdeveloped, functioned or malfunctioned, and fallen victim to unacceptable injustices, over the last 50 years.

All Characters portrayed in "Masses of Asses" are fictitious and any resemblance they might bear to real persons is purely coincidental

JF

CONTENTS

1. IMPASSE — 5
2. EN ROUTE — 13
3. PLOTS AND PLOYS — 24
4. THE "INTERVIEW" — 42
5. COMPREHENSIVE *EDIFICATION* — 47
6. TRAVEL BROADENS THE MIND — 69
7. CHANCE ENCOUNTERS — 79
8. EGOS — 93
9. FRENCH FOR THE FRY — 98
10. A NICHE FOR EVERYONE — 103
11. *DEUS EX MACHINA* — 112
12. PETER PISSPOT — 117
13. SOME MOTHERS DO 'AVE 'EM — 123
14. ENGLISH *DOWN THE TUBE* — 140
15. LADY LUCK EXPELLED — 151
16. THE BUREAUCRATIC BOGEYMAN — 159
17. SITTING ON THE PERENNIAL FENCE — 166
18. THE CHICKEN OR THE EGG? — 182

Chapter 1
IMPASSE

A morning in 1974. Candlish could hear them coming as soon as they turned into the long corridor and were still ten rooms away. They came like an avalanche, and like an avalanche they swept aside or sent spinning any unfortunates who happened to be caught in their relentless path; not till they arrived at his door did the stampede come to an untidy stop and change to a mêlée in which its leaders were pitched against the wall at the end of the cul-de-sac by those in their rear. IIIC had arrived, and with them the acrid smell of sweat and of linen long overdue renewal. The new darlings of the great new educational era were at last being given their chance.

"Right, go in and fill up the seats from the front."

An order which inspired a second charge — for the back.

Candlish left the door ajar and opened more windows.

The mad rush to get there might have been interpreted, by those who know no better, as impatience to make up for lost time, as enthusiasm to accrue the knowledge long denied them under an uncaring selective system; in fact running was one of the things they could do and when others were around they never missed the opportunity to show that they had mastered the art.

Candlish was new to this business, never having been off-loaded with such as them before; in his sixteen years of teaching he had espied them only from afar, which was near enough; and had heard from demented colleagues how damned lucky he was to be a Modern Language teacher and spared the very bottom of the pile. But not any longer.

Once they were all seated or, more accurately, sprawled over desks and chairs in seemingly impossible postures which tended to belie any limits to the stretchability of the human anatomy, they gawped at this unknown quantity they thought they had seen somewhere before but couldn't be quite sure.

For a second or two Candlish scrutinized the assembled throng. And wished he hadn't, for the facial expressions were not all that encouraging.

"I am Mr Candlish and you are here for a course on what is called French Studies. You will ..."

"Diz that mean ye'll be learnin' us fur tae speak French, sur?"

"Do not interrupt. Just listen. You will *not* be learning the French language apart from ..."

"That's no' fair, sur. Nearly a' the ither classes git French."

As if he needed to be reminded. And considering the nightmare which that had created, he inwardly thanked God that those in front of him had been deemed even by the great social levellers to fall just that little bit short of being sufficiently endowed to share in such enlightenment. For the time being at any rate; ominous whispers were going the rounds.

"Look, I told you not to interrupt. You will not be learning the French language apart from the occasional word or phrase. But you will learn about France itself, a little of its history and its geography, about its main towns and its industries, its people and how they live. Now as I have no idea how much you already know about the country I am going to ask you one or two very simple questions."

Blank stares. No apprehension. No apprehension when you are blissfully aware of your own ignorance.

"First question. And don't all shout the answer at once. Put up your hands. Suppose we were travelling from Glentilloch to France by train or by car, in which general direction would we go?"

Don't all shout out at once? If anything the blankness of the stares intensified. And no heads bowed in embarrassment. Embarrassment, like apprehension, never came into it.

"Well, would we go North or South or East or West?"

"Whut wid we want tae gaun tae France fur, sur?"

Candlish did his best to retain his equanimity.

"That's not the point. Oh come on, would we go North or South or East or West?"

West was the only direction in which some of them ever travelled. West was the way you went to get to Ibrox or Parkhead. The pupil, clad in a green and white jersey, must have picked that fact up sometime on one of his safaris to The Jungle.

"Christ, how the hell am I going to survive this lot?" Candlish squirmed at the thought of having them twice a week until the end of term. Yet he had no other option but to continue, to go through the motions until the bell heralded escape both for him and them.

"No, you would head South. And which stretch of water would you have to cross?"

"The Clyde, sur!"

Candlish allowed himself a rueful smile. The boy was right, of course, if unwittingly, if a narrow river by the A74 could be described as a stretch of water.

"Yes, you would have to cross the Clyde. But by a stretch of water I mean a broad stretch of water with no bridges, where you need a boat, quite a big boat; where you would have to cross the sea."

"A ken! Th'Atlantic Ocean, sur. That's a sea, sur. In the Queen Mary, sur."

"Let's try again."

"Try whut again?"

He tried again:

"Who can tell me where London is?"

"That's whaur Arsenal play, sur, an' they're an English team, so it must be in England!"

Good policy, taking one cautious step at a time, groping your way towards an ultimate and unerring conclusion. Pity when the clues ran out.

"But how do you get to England, to London?"

"Git oan a bus or a train wi' England or London written oan it. Or mebbe ye could flee, A dinnae ken."

Not surpricingly, after such a revealing performance by those who were considered to be the least uneducable in IIIC, he found that not a single member of the class had even the haziest notion of either the map of Scotland or of the UK, not to mention the Continent of Europe. France was merely a word some of them seemed to think they had heard, no doubt in connection with that country's participation in the World Cup. But de Gaulle? What team did he play for? Couldn't have been one of God's gifts to the world of football.

Thankfully the bell rang to signal the end of the period and they stormed out just as they had come in, desperate to get to their next port of call, desperate to adorn more unsuspecting seats with their restless bottoms and have someone else with an Honours degree wonder what the hell he or she was doing there.

* * *

For the next lesson, three days later, having already had their bellyful of France without so far having reached it, they arrived perceptibly slower, but still in the form of a cavalry charge. That was how IIIC did things. They knew no other way.

They were fidgeting and throwing balls of paper and bawling "Fuck ye!" at each other only minutes after Candlish had started. He brought them to order, or to something approaching order.

For this second attempt at "French Studies" he had prepared the ground, with the object of giving them something tangible to do and hence to keep them reasonably quiet — if they assimilated some knowledge so much the better. He had drawn a rough but sufficiently accurate outline of Europe and the coastline of North Africa on the blackboard (which was in fact a greenboard on which you used yellow chalk — a great innovation and all due to the new breed of dedicated educational psychologists who, after extensive and painstaking research, were now almost certain that yellow on green provided a more powerful motivating factor for pupils than white on black. Such mind-boggling breakthroughs demonstrated in unequivocal fashion the strength of the support of those toiling in the background for those engaged at the chalkface). Candlish had drawn in national borders and overprinted the names of the countries in block letters and their respective capitals in small. They were told to copy the whole thing into the big fat notebooks which had cost the local authority 80 pence each. Although so far unused in the classroom these were showing unmistakable signs of wear and tear. They had served as efficient head-thumpers in the school bus.

"That's ma pincil ye've got, ya rotten bastard! A ken it fae ma chew marks."

"Please, sur, A havnae got a pincil. McGonchie stealt it fae me last week, sur."

"Ma wee brither took mine, sur."

"*You* got oany pincils, sur?"

Prepared for such an eventuality Candlish distributed the required equipment from an assortment he regularly picked up from desks and floor.

"Please, sur, Tookie's got a better yin than me. S'no' fair, sur."

"Oh shut up, the lot of you, and get on with it. Another word and I'll knock someone's head off."

"Ye cannae touch us, sur. S'no' allowed oany mair."

They might not know much, but they knew their "rights", and where these were concerned they never missed a trick; and already seemed to sense that no matter what, a benevolent Welfare State, whatever that was, would see them through.

But the change in Candlish's attitude had not passed unnoticed. Eyes oscillated between greenboard and exercise books as their would-be mentor glowered at them, then started to move from desk to desk.

So great was the degree of inaccuracy that he all but laughed out hysterically. In some cases the Channel was as broad as the Central Pacific ("The page wisnae big enough, sur."), and in others the UK looked like an eel hell-bent on wriggling its way towards the Americas; even where a recognisable approximation of the perimeters of Europe had been achieved Paris and Berlin had somehow switched positions, Rome found itself in what vaguely looked like Norway and the toe of Italy lay on Libyan soil, cutting the eastern Mediterranean off from direct maritime contact with the Atlantic and posing problems for the Cyprus potato and Jaffa orange industries.

The copying had taken up half the period. Time for a change. So he showed them large coloured pictures of the beauties of Paris. No good. Not to be compared with Page 3 or Elvis in full cry, or Georgie Best in full flight.

More fidgeting. More "Whut's the time?" Important to them, the time. "Whaur'ye gaun the nicht?" "Ye oany fags?" "Shut yer mooth!"

They had had enough of concentration for one day and this time were more difficult to quell. But expectancy was raised a few degrees when "Skin" McNeil, he of diminutive build and pasty of face, piped up:

"Sur, can ye no' tell us a' aboot the War, fightin' an' a' that?"

They knew there had been a war! TV did have its advantages, glamorised and falsified as most of the films were (he suspected they never watched documentaries). And why should he not tell them about it? France had been traumatically involved, the whole of Europe metamorphosed by it. Such a topic was arguably within his remit. Christ, who cared anyway? The buggers had to be kept quiet somehow.

"How much do you know about the Second World War?"

"Why wiz it ca'd the *Second* World War, sur?"

"No' much, sur, only whut John Wayne an' them did, sur. You tell us, sur!"

"Well, first of all, can anyone give me the names of any of the countries which fought against the Allies?"

"Whut's All... Allies, sur?"

"An ally is a nation which fights on the same side as another nation. In other words, name a country which fought on Germany's side?"

"A ken, sur! Russia, sur!"

"Well, tell me, who was Britain's prime minister during the greater part of the War?"

They couldn't think of a name, any name, to shout out.

"Wur you in the War, sur? Wuz ye a commando, sur?"

"No, I wasn't a commando. I was with Bomber Command."

"Whut wiz that, sur? Wiz that no' commandos that threw bombs at them, sur?"

He had never known the past tense of the verb "to be" to have so many variations. Yet that, he supposed, was a mere bagatelle in a great yawning abyss of scholastic emptiness. But he didn't bother to explain; after all, this Bomber Command outfit, whatever it was, could not have played much of a part in the fighting, otherwise John Wayne would have been in it.

* * *

That same evening Candlish decided to attend a senior football match in which the home team, Glentilloch Thistle, were entertaining a side from the Glasgow area. A little winger, one of the first coloured players to be seen in Scotland, was causing the homesters no end of bother with his fast dribbling runs and accurate crosses into the goalmouth. A joy to watch. Not for everyone, though:

"Fuck ye, ya wee black bastard. It's time ye stopped fur yer bunch o' bananas."

No mistaking that voice. Candlish turned his head and

confirmed the presence of Prentice of IIIC who, judging by his greasy pallor and manifold spots — the direct consequence of his regular diet of burgers and sausages and chips, or of sausages and burgers and chips, or of chips and sausages and burgers — looked as if he could have done with some fresh fruit himself.

During the walk home he pondered, not on the game itself, but on the elevated company he had to thole. Going to the match had been in large measure a means of escape, but they were there too. They were everywhere. If he went to the river for some fishing of an evening they would no doubt come crawling out from beneath the stones. It was at moments like this, and obviously there were going to be many more moments like this, that he wished he had transferred from wartime bomber to civilian airliner. Now it was far too late. He was out of touch and he was far too damned old.

Damn it all, how could human beings be separated by such an unbridgeable gap? Human beings! Same more or less physically, same organs, same limbs, same basic instincts, but the varying contents of their skulls! Yet the trendy disciples of parity in all things had got away with it. The gulf existed only because the poor wee bastards had been educationally underprivileged. But not any more. The New Order would put all that right in no time. Although still in its infancy its efficacy was being proven already in "seats of learning" all over the country.

Anyone who believed that ...

Chapter 2
EN ROUTE

October 1946.

The ruins of Dortmund on a Monday, Lancashire's Lytham St Anne's for demobilisation on Tuesday, attendance at an introduction in German to the *Sturm und Drang* period of literature at St Andrews two days later; for Iain Candlish, DFC, the transition from an officers' mess in the Ruhr to a lecture-room in "the auld grey toon by the northern sea", from the blue uniform of the RAF to the scarlet gown of Scotland's most ancient university, had been brutal in its suddenness.

As the professor, not of recent vintage himself, droned on in the language of Goethe — and of Hitler — with an accent somewhat less than true Teutonic, reading out notes unaltered over four decades, Candlish found concentration elusive as he sat uncomfortably in an ambience so familiar, yet so unfamiliar, after an absence of six years; of six action-packed years which seemed to have gone in a flash, yet during which he had experienced more than any human being should be asked to face in a lifetime, or in a dozen lifetimes if that is not rather a silly thing to say; six years of excitement which had so easily become turmoil and frenzy, of living on a knife edge, of getting to know a type of fear which gnawed at your very entrails during, before and after every no holds barred battle with the might of Goering's air defence in the night skies of Germany, years in which he had participated in the massive destruction of that nation's cities and in the massive killing of her population, and had seen his own friends and comrades decimated in the process; then, pitched literally head-first into the deprivations and miseries of a Stalag Luft, there had followed the euphoria of liberation, and thereafter the grim and harrowing task he had performed in cemeteries and fields and woods throughout the Ruhr and Rhineland Westphalia. A little more of which in due course.

Now all that was over. In a strange sort of way he felt he was being reborn, and he knew that the rebirth would be a difficult one. But then all of life was difficult and perhaps worthless if it wasn't.

* * *

It might be fitting to pause once more, go back a little further, and to elaborate somewhat on the various steps taken along the path which was to lead Candlish ultimately to those demoralising confrontations with Class IIIC in Glentilloch High School in 1974.

At the age of eleven he had won a bursary from his primary school in Perthshire to one of Scotland's best known fee-paying secondaries. After he had obtained a commendable group of passes in the Senior Leaving Certification Examination (the nomenclature in those days) his parents were advised that he was definitely university material and had determined without further ado that to such an institution he would go. Although aided to a certain extent by grants from philanthropists such as Andrew Carnegie, they found the undertaking to be a tough one financially and personal sacrifices had to be made. But in the true traditions of educationally minded Scottish parents these were accepted willingly.

So, at the age of seventeen plus in October 1936, just six months after the Führer had made his first tentative move to test European reaction by re-occupying the Rhineland, Candlish departed the paternal roof for St Andrews and embarked on a course leading to an Honours degree in French and German.

Having successfully completed his first two sessions, by which time Hitler had annexed Austria, Candlish arrived in Nuremberg — in those early days he preferred the strong expressiveness of German to the delicate subtleties of French — to begin his third year of study. He had hardly settled in his new surroundings when German troops marched into the Sudetenland and then took over the whole of Czechoslovakia in March 1939. It wasn't a situation which was conducive to the concentration required for academic work for he also saw with his own perceptive eyes — not that perceptive eyes were in any way necessary — what was afoot in the Third Reich itself: the shameful hounding of the Jews, the ultra-smart and awe-inspiring SS, symbolising in indubitable fashion the superiority of the "Aryan" breed, the arrogant, strutting Wehrmacht, the ubiquitous presence of the Gestapo and the icy grip in which it held all the nation's subjects. And then just after his departure from Germany and just before the commencement of his final year back in St Andrews, Churchill's "gathering storm" finally burst when the sizzling fuse reached the waiting keg and the world exploded. As was the lot of so many of his generation his plans for the future were rudely interrupted by the more grandiose aspirations of the moustached gentleman from Linz.

In that era the great majority of young men became infused on such occasions with a deep sense of patriotism and a willingness to serve, an attitude which few of their children and grandchildren would understand and which many would now deplore as xenophobic and misguided. But it wasn't considered to be misguided then; and for his own part Candlish had seen enough to know that this was a war which had to be fought and which had to be won.

With scant enthusiasm for the Army (his spell in the Officers' Training Corps while at secondary school had put paid to that) but with an interest in flying ever since his father had treated him to a five-shilling trip at Renfrew Airport on his fourteenth birthday, he immediately offered his services for aircrew and, after a rigorous medical examination — his mental capacity was not in doubt — was accepted, gained his pilot's wings about a year later and eventually carried out a number of operations in a Wellington before being badly wounded over Kiel. That was followed by a long period of hospitalization and convalescence, retraining and conversion to the four-engined Stirling and then to the Lancaster. He had miraculously survived more than thirty incursions into Europe, mainly to Germany, and knew he was living on borrowed time two or three times over when, on that blackest night in Bomber Command's history (113 aircraft and over 600 airmen lost on March 30/31, 1944) Lady Luck finally deserted him while on the last lap to Nuremberg — of all places — but he managed to bail out safely with two other members of his crew. The four others did not make it.

After fifteen months in a prisoner of war camp, where he partly nullified both frustration and boredom in the study of any classic German literature he could lay his hands on, sometimes obtaining forbidden texts by Jewish writers from stupid guards prepared to risk a posting to the Eastern Front, or worse, in exchange for some comestible or nicotinic luxuries from his Red Cross parcels, he was liberated in May 1945 and sent back forthwith to the UK — as a passenger in a Lancaster. Redundant as aircrew and eager to return to Germany to become orally proficient and to read as much as possible before resuming his university classes, he volunteered to become an Investigations Officer with the RAF Missing Research and Enquiry Service, established soon after the end of hostilities for the purpose of tracking down the bodies of the thousands of aircrew whose ultimate fate — and their last resting-places if these existed (in several cases there was nothing left to bury) — were unknown; this had entailed the attempted identification of former colleagues by sifting through their putrefying remains to find personal items such as mascots or letters or rings. In September 1946 he applied for Class B demobilization to enable him to return to university and, as we now know, he had become a student again almost at once.

French was still regarded in that epoch as a sort of third classic, considered to fall not far short of Latin itself as a test of linguistic ability and taught, as were all modern languages, in the same formal and uninspiring manner (practise in conversation, surely the main *raison d'etre* for learning any spoken tongue, appeared to be deemed undesirable). It was also the most common language on the curriculum of secondary schools — with about 90% of able pupils studying it compared to perhaps 8% taking German and 2% Spanish if the latter were available. The lecturer at the first French class Candlish attended was a mere strip of a lass who had just graduated the previous year and displayed obvious nervousness on being confronted by such a mass of gaping humanity. Her uneasiness visibly increased when her opening remark — "Today I am going to deal with Molière and his plot" — was greeted by a loud and resonant response from an unstudent-looking character in the body of the throng:

"Good old Molière! Dig for victory!"

The disrupter, Candlish learned later, was an ex-commando whose skull was held together with metal plates, and who found it only natural, even in the venerable atmosphere of an ancient university, to give vent to the unrestrained bawdiness so typical of the camaraderie amongst fighting men who regularly find themselves in desperate situations. Candlish had been no stranger to these himself and welcomed the undisciplined but spirited intrusion, as it helped to make him feel less embarrassed in a group largely predominated by baby-faced youngsters, most of them out of their own backyards for the very first time and their only sight of the world so far their journey to St Andrews by bus or train. Yet ex-servicemen were there in a small but conspicuous minority — the forerunners of what would be latter dubbed "mature students". Some of them did not possess the requisite entrance qualifications but, by dint of their war records and of what they had learned of the world, had been given a chance by the more generous of the ruling academic bodies which decided on such matters. Their contribution to the general environs did no harm either, for their numbers included many wise beyond their years who bore the inevitable scars of war, both physical and mental. A fair proportion of them were unfortunately to fall by the wayside, and soon, the reason often being their inability to settle down and cope with a régime which could hardly have stood in more blatant contrast to the one they had just renounced.

Candlish got through the intellectual marathon of his final year, which came at last to a halt in May 1948 with a whole week of exams — two three-hour papers in Honours French and German each day from Monday until Friday and one on Saturday morning. On completing the final inquisition he had gone half-way along North Street on his way back to his lodgings before he realised he was walking in the wrong direction.

* * *

Then the results: a good Second Class in the two languages. He was quite satisfied, and particularly so since the Faculty of Arts at St Andrews was not renowned for awarding Firsts.

What now? What to do? Where to go? After making several enquiries and arranging interviews with university officials and doing a lot of thinking he decided, for various reasons, that he would become a teacher; first of all, from what he had heard from different sources, a degree in modern languages opened few vocational doors, unless these languages were Russian or Oriental. Apparently about all you could do with French and German was to pass your knowledge of them on to the nation's children. You went to school, learned them, studied them in depth at university, then went back to school and taught them to the up-coming generation who, if gifted in that sphere, did exactly the same. A vicious, perhaps a pointless, circle. But his decision was far from being merely a pragmatic one: teaching would provide the means of retaining his languages which, if unused, were all too quickly forgotten; further, having witnessed in graphic and chilling fashion during his sojourn in Nuremberg what the poisoning of young minds had achieved, and was still achieving while he was there — under the influence of an odious little Minister of Propaganda who was nothing less than the equivalent of a Head

Teacher with the entire population as his school — he had arrived at the firm conclusion, idealistic and pompous as it sounded, that teachers were entrusted with the moulding of the seed corn entrusted to them and to a large extent held the future welfare of their country in their hands. Surely it was the most important job of the lot, because without them there would be nothing, no scientists, no doctors, no lawyers — and no teachers; and there was something else: he felt sick at heart of all the destruction he had seen and some of which he himself had sown; and felt an urge to direct his efforts to something constructive, to build up rather than to knock down.

Therefore, blissfully unaware of what lay round the corner in the field he had chosen, and not foreseeing — how could he? — how it would be transformed once the newly-formed Welfare State got into top gear, and then overdrive, he put his name on the list for the next session's intake to the Teachers' Training College in Dundee, not knowing the very name would prove to be something of a misnomer.

In conjunction with the course leading to the Teachers' Secondary Certificate (most of the classes were held in Dundee every Monday) he studied for the University Diploma in Education at St Andrews. This consisted of Psychology and the History and Theory of Education, which were at least interesting (although all you needed to do was to read the prescribed books, which the lecturers had obviously done) and the scenario somewhat more edifying than the pantomime written and enacted by the pedagogic illuminaries on stage in Dundee.

Some of the latter performed in St Andrews (no doubt a welcome escape for them from the penitentiary-like building and atmosphere of their headquarters on the other side of the Tay). One such class went under the name of Religious Education and was held in a quaint old room in St Mary's College off South Street (Principal the Very Rev. George Duncan, chaplain to Douglas Haig during the First World War, which must have given him much food for thought in later years when all the facts came to light), where long shafts of mote-rich sunlight were lazily projected from the multi-coloured, saint-adorned windows; and where the students were subjected to the galvanizing utterances of a well-meaning but unwittingly comical little individual who might in fact have gone a long way by just being himself if music halls had not been going out of fashion: "Holy Horace" or, more usually, "Holy Horry", was endowed with a snooker-ball-smooth pate which dazzled anyone who risked casting it a glance when it was captured by the sun's rays; but that was by no means his sole eye-catching attribute: his ears were of the wide-open taxi doors variety, but even they paled into insignificance when compared with the most pronounced and largest rabbit teeth any of them had ever seen, not even on a rabbit. And these had effects which went far beyond the visual, for each time he attempted to emphasise a word or phrase — a frequent ploy with him — this was reinforced by a long-range salvo of divine saliva. Hence the main reason why the front seats were never occupied and for the gratitude of his unwilling disciples for the existence of less precarious pews on which they could deposit their posteriors.

    The combination of the warm sunshine and the dreary tones and the fatuous jargon (designed, they suspected, to uplift his own spirits rather than theirs) constituted a perfect recipe to induce slumber and invariably each and every one of his supposed listeners, unless they were suffering from toothache or some equally painful affliction, fell sound asleep; and so engrossed was His Reverence in his delivery (in any case his eyes were raised eternally upwards) that he didn't even notice, not even when one or two of them started to saw some wood. Or perhaps he thought he was giving one of his pulsating sermons in church and expected nothing else.

    Candlish, an admirer of Albert Camus and inclined towards agnosticism, wondered what the hell all this had to do with the teaching of French and German.

Another leading member of the Dundee troupe, a female lecturer in Health and Hygiene, dealt with things they had all learned from their grannies and announced them as startling discoveries: most classroom windows should be opened when it was hot and most of them closed when it was cold; pupils should be made to sit upright in their seats; they should not be allowed to bring wet coats into the classroom, and so on and so on. Candlish, feeling both humiliated and angry, rose to his feet and interrupted her apologetically, saying he thought he must have come to the wrong room:

"Oh no," she retorted in complete innocence, "you must all pass in Heath and Hygiene. So important for the children's welfare. I can't stress that enough."

Then one day she went completely haywire and blushingly stuttered her way through a talk on adolescent male and female pupil relationships, which would have brought few blushes to the faces of future pupils who were at that moment still toddling around after their mothers or not yet conceived.

All that nonsense was bad enough, but Candlish and those who had boarded the same boat became quite appalled when they attended lectures in which they expected to be taught guidelines that were both unambiguous and informative: those on Modern Language teaching methods. Yet they were anything but, and presented in such a vague and haphazard and unconvincing manner as to suggest — no, rather to confirm — that their so-called instructors had themselves spent little time out there where it all happened. If they had, then their results must have been abysmally poor; perhaps that was why they had turned to lecturing — not an unheard of means of escape for those who unhappily bumbled their way through each school period or were hopeless disciplinarians — or both, since the two failings were invariably indiscerptible. Such a state of affairs added a new twist to the old saying, "Those who can't, teach" — "and those who can't teach, teach teachers."

The lecturer permanently allotted to Candlish and his group was in fact the Head of the Department and he did not make much of a favourable impression at the first meeting and even less so during those that followed. Mind you he didn't get off to a good start on entering the room because his bizarre appearance tended to re-awaken memories of their recent visit to Holy Horace, although the contours were all different, and caused them to wonder if such caricatures were the norm amongst the staff of Training Colleges. An exceptionally tall, pencil-thin individual with a face a foot long, upsettingly lugubrious and with a voice to match, his entire demeanour seemed to have been tailored to mirror the fact that all was not right with the world and his physiognomy would surely have disintegrated forthwith had he ever got anywhere near forcing a smile (not the slightest danger of the real thing). Those to whom Mr Doom and Gloom was supposed to impart the proven tenets of modern language methodology refused to believe their ears when, in all seriousness — no need for him to strain himself in that direction — he stressed what he claimed to be an all-essential point: in handling a class you had to display a sense of humour; have a laugh with the little blighters (he said "with your protégés") now and again; show them you were human and get them on your side; nor was there anything wrong with the occasional tasteful joke if the opportunity presented itself. One couldn't imagine the opportunity presenting itself very often when he was around.

So pathetically poor were his "lectures", in which he stuttered his way from one contradictory statement to another, and so hypercritical was he of his students' attempts to teach a class during practice spells at Madras College (the senior secondary in St Andrews) where his totally confused victims found themselves subjected to the embarrassing and unrealistic situation of having to take over a group of thirty fourteen-year olds late on a Friday afternoon in the presence of their normal teacher and of course of Mr Doom and Gloom himself, in addition to three or four of their fellow-sufferers (also there as critics for later discussion) that the prospective teachers, absolutely fed up with his attitude and his apparently sadistic pleasure in tearing their efforts apart, challenged him to give them a demonstration lesson to show them how it should be done. Nothing doing. In fact they were severely rebuked for making such an outrageous and impertinent suggestion. Pity, because for one thing they were dying to hear one of his jokes; and if it caused the concrete features to crack that too would have been an experience not to be missed.

But at the end of the course each and every one of them passed with plenty to spare and gained their open sesames to the second oldest profession on earth and, they were told, the noblest of them all. They knew they could no more teach a class than Doom and Gloom could have taught at a school for comics. But both primaries and secondaries were crying out for bodies ...

Perhaps all TCs were not like that and he and his colleagues had just been unfortunate, but in any case it was glaringly obvious that the poor buggers would have to learn their trade as they went along. Candlish thought back to his own meticulous flying training and couldn't suppress a sardonic smile: Christ, if the RAF had prepared its recruits along similar lines we would have lost the bloody war.

Chapter 3
PLOTS AND PLOYS

In those immediate post-war years schools suffered from a general dearth of teaching staff, especially in the Sciences and Mathematics (and later in Modern Languages), a situation doomed to worsen throughout the decades to come when successive governments, whether Conservative or Labour, proved beyond a shadow of doubt that education occupied a lowly rung on their ladder of priorities. Consequently an entrant to the profession could more or less pick any town, or at least any area, in which to live. For Candlish the time was ripe to arrange other matters as well and on completion of his teacher training (we'll be generous and call it that) he and his lady friend of nearly four years standing (an ex-WAAF to whom he had become engaged just days before becoming an unwilling guest of Hermann Goering) decided they would delay no longer in taking the final step. This they did quickly and quietly and without indulging in all the established rituals normally associated with such a ceremony; all the blahblah, such as the joint cutting of a wedding cake and the accompanying applause — as if this was an act requiring consummate skill — they regarded as childish nonsense and would have none of these goings-on despite the agonized pleas from both mothers.

They were attracted by a vacancy for a teacher of French and German in Abergarvie, a town conveniently situated just north of the great expanse of land whose multifarious regions were to be grouped together some years later under the humdrum title "Central". It was a place which offered Candlish at close hand the opportunity to indulge in his main leisure pursuit, gamefishing, and Eileen plenty of scope for her love of painting scenes by river and loch; and she could do it in her husband's company.

He applied for the post and was granted it without interview.

That was what normally happened around that time: education authorities were only too grateful that someone with the requisite paper qualifications was available. Although that did not infer the candidate possessed automatic teaching ability or even potential teaching ability, who cared? They had filled another post with a body that could breathe and walk and if they were able to report that a school carried a full complement of staff then they could smugly preen themselves in public. They had done a fine job. The most stupid farmer in creation would never have tholed the grazing of promising pasture land by a herd containing a number of dried-up cows but there existed no such thing as an equivalent form of husbandry in institutions where one would have expected much weight to be placed on a similar high level of production. It is difficult to think of any other occupation in which the essential requirements — in this case the ability to teach and the ability to maintain discipline — were taken into so little account. Granted that it was no easy task to assess an outright beginner, and not fair to do so until he had settled in (I should of course say "until *he* or *she* had settled in," but such a juxtaposition would occur frequently and the text would begin to sound like an official document, so feminists are respectfully requested not to regard the future omission of *she* as a glaring example of "male chauvinism," to use that overused and now hackneyed term, but merely as a means to retain a more readable form of language. It could be argued, after all, that men of both sexes are not all that rare in the profession); oh yes, there was a so-called "probationary period", during which a member of the Inspectorate came perhaps a couple of times to observe the performance of a raw recruit, but the fact remained that you could carry on year after year being the lousiest teacher in the world and unless you sexually interfered with a pupil or half killed him retention of your position continued to be unassailable. Never in his entire career did Candlish know of a single case where a teacher was booted out into the street for sheer incompetence in the classroom. But how could they be, when these same streets were already being combed for any Tom, Dick or Harriet who knew a little about a subject and was welcomed as a heaven-sent find to fill one of the growing number of gaps? Inconceivable? Oh no! Examples later.

    The combined financial resources of Candlish and his wife fell far short of the sum necessary for the minimum deposit on a mortgage — a lot harder to procure around the middle of the century than towards its end. Furthermore the waiting list for local authority houses was a long one and these, in any case, were available only to "key workers", a category which excluded those entrusted with the education of the young. When Candlish went to see if any exceptions were made (for ex-servicemen, for instance) he was told by a minor automaton, brimful of his own meagre importance, that he found it rather surprising that a teacher, of all people, should expect to be given a council house. My God, they had to attract essential tradesmen such as joiners, bricklayers and plasterers. Yes, and scavengers. You couldn't do without scavengers. Teachers? The Council had to get everything into perspective. But the couple did derive some sort of negative consolation from the fact that they were not exactly enamoured with the idea of being domiciled in a new scheme often resonant with war cries and already dubbed by many affluent Abergarvians as "Red Indian Country". So furnished lodgings had to be found, unfortunately at a prohibitive price and creating a financial impasse since there was little left of Candlish's take-home salary of well under £50 per month to accrue the deposit required by the building societies. And this was still an era in which the main function of a married woman was that of a housewife, even if she had no children and plenty of time on her hands; accordingly no thought of Eileen taking a job, and just as well perhaps because her previous banking experience (after leaving the WAAF) would have been useless: such institutions were not in the habit of employing married women if they could help it; married women could become pregnant, and that caused disruption. Not that the same policy applied to schools. In fact the system would all but have collapsed without them and mothers-to-be were often begged to remain at their posts until the last possible moment, with the inevitable outcome that in cases of premature birth or where the doctors had got the delivery date wrong, there existed every likelihood that a child could be dropped in the staffroom — or in the classroom. On some occasions it must have come damned near to that. And human reproduction did not then figure on the biology syllabus; perhaps a great pity, as the chance could have presented itself for the pupils to observe a practical demonstration of the real thing. That would have got the old spinsters' chins wagging as never before. And chins can't wag more than that.

    The couple managed to rent a room (and the share of the kitchen — not, fortunately, in this case a recipe for disaster) in a largish house in rather an attractive part of the town. Their landlady, a widow, displayed a certain amount of eccentricity but was cooperative enough and respected their need of privacy.

    Abergarvie Academy was one of those moderately-sized Scottish senior secondaries set in a moderately-sized town, and, as was typical of such schools, still staffed by a preponderance of pre-war graduates and with a long and generally commendable record of teaching efficiency. It stood in direct contrast to Abergarvie High School, situated a good distance away on the other side of the river and the home of the "also-rans" whose "Control Examination" (taken in the final year of primary) results allegedly proved that they had not been endowed with the necessary amount of grey matter to suggest that they were Senior Leaving Certificate material and were thus branded on admission to the junior secondary as educational failures by the population at large. The teachers there too were apt to be regarded as of inferior professional calibre since most of them who had studied academic subjects possessed only Ordinary Degrees, which meant, in that era, that they were not qualified to coach for the SLC Examination, and tended to languish in such schools, uninspired and unappreciated, their main function being, realistically, to police each week day most of the teenage riff-raff who lived in Abergarvie. (One of the members of that school's English Department, a sexagenarian called Bob Stewart, whom Candlish met regularly on the river, told him one evening that he had finally relinquished his last vestige of hope. One of his textbooks had been defaced on its frontispiece with the words, in large capitals: STEWART IS A COUNT. "I was momentarily flattered," he said, "until of course I realised they can't even spell the words they use most.") Those parents, often of professional status themselves, and who could not bear the thought of their not-too-bright offspring stagnating and socially deteriorating in the High School as they continually brushed shoulders with the morons and the yobs, subjected them, while they were in Primary 7, to a rigorous diet of stereotyped IQ and English Language tests; and so it could happen, and did, that their performance in the "Control" exaggerated their true ability and gained them acceptance into the Academy; such aspirants for the most part floundered unhappily in the early years of the Senior Secondary and left it at the then statutory leaving age of 15 with no certificates to their name, but having been part of a more civilised ambience. Yet such wastage was small and at least the authorities erred on the right side. But the day was not far off when they would go off the rails completely and err totally; when they would climb to the dizziest heights of educational beneficence and expound the theory that all were equal; perhaps they were all equal in the eyes of God but the exponents of the coming fashion refused to acknowledge the blunt fact that down here on this godless earth things rarely work that way.

    Candlish's Principal Teacher was John Naithsmith, a middle-aged Glaswegian who saw everything in black and white and brooked little argument about anything. He asked Candlish to stay on for a few minutes after 4 o'clock on the first day of the new session and told him categorically that if he thought he had learned anything at TC he would be best to forget it. Thank the Lord for that. Not much of a problem there.

"The main requirements in teaching," said Naithsmith, "are a strong personality, plenty of drilling to knock the stuff into them and to keep them on their toes, continual hard work — and sound common sense. Either you have the requisite qualities, or have them to some degree, or you don't have them at all. The number of the plus factors you possess determines how much of a success or a failure you will be. A strong personality invariably implies strict discipline. The two go hand in hand. Results are all that matter, and I don't really care how they are achieved. Any soft ha'porth who gets trampled into the floorboards is an absolute liability to the Department and won't reign here for long if I have anything to do with it." (Candlish learned the next day that the vacancy he had filled had arisen following Naithsmith's long and ultimately successful efforts to have his previous occupant transferred across the river to Abergarvie High, where he "would do less harm").

It took no more than a week or two for Candlish to learn that his boss's methods were even more draconian than he had made them sound, and that his more imaginative senior pupils had modified "Naithsmith" to the not too dissimilar *Nazareth*. But their fellow-sufferers of Christian bent — and there were a few — vehemently rejected this appellation as a form of the grossest blasphemy and suggested that the short *Nazi* would be more appropriate and less irreverent and would offend no-one who came under his tutelage whatever their religious persuasion.

Although conscious of his own greenness as a beginner and not yet sure whether he would make the grade or not, Candlish did not altogether welcome what appeared to be an ultra-harsh attitude on Naithsmith's part. Of course you needed discipline, but his Principal's conception of it conjured up an atmosphere you might expect to find in a detention centre rather than a classroom. The imparting of knowledge through fear did not seem to be the right way, for it implied that its acquisition must be something unpleasant and unnatural. The outpouring of sweat — his as well as theirs — he could accept, but there would certainly be no outpouring of blood such as he had witnessed on many wrists at his own highly acclaimed senior secondary, where fear and punishment or fear of punishment had too often been the weapon used in too many armouries to counteract wrong answers or minor infractions. At the same time he was not unforeseeing enough to realise that a situation might arise where moderate corporal punishment might be both justified and salutory, though not salutory, he suspected, to himself. Somehow it seemed to be an admission of failure, the coward's way out. True discipline, he felt, could be won only through mutual respect and mutual endeavour. It was a two-way business, with none of the "Them and Us" syndrome which was bedevilling the country's industrial relations. Pupils had to view their teacher as a caring ally, not a sadistic foe, and the sole aim had to be complete co-operation in an orderly but relaxed atmosphere. Each side could see the funny side of things when the occasion arose, and enjoy it, but when Candlish stopped laughing they too had to stop and serious work would resume; a bit of hilarity would never be allowed to trigger off general disruption and the end of any effective work for more than a few seconds; no getting into an irreversible slide on a slippery slope.

    This was the attitude he adopted and it rarely failed him. It rarely failed him because he was fortunate enough to be what he was, in possessing the indefinable and elusive personality traits which many lacked and which could not be taught. As Naithsmith had said, you either had it or you didn't, although the latter's ideas on the subject, with his emphasis on sheer intimidation, were not, and he hoped, never would be, his own. At the same time he was well aware he was dealing with selected pupils who in the main enjoyed the advantage of good home backgrounds and were interested and ambitious, and from what he had heard of goings-on in the High School, where the majority of the inmates were innately anti-teacher, the only effective means of control was the big whip. So those were still halcyon days for such as him before the nascent band of do-gooders swelled into a great all-conquering army and fired a devastating salvo of crazily idealistic ammunition of which the inevitable outcome would be the type of scenario to which we were treated in Chapter I, and others, alas, which we shall describe in due course.

Candlish gradually found his way, proceeding cautiously and putting to full use the trial and error technique, filing off what he considered to be rough corners in his approach, displaying firmness towards his pupils but never ill-temper or nastiness, and finally settling into an established routine. After a month or two Naithsmith no longer came in to observe him in action and that, he concluded, was as sure a sign as any that he had set a good course; but a course à la Candlish rather than à la Naithsmith.

The latter, not surprisingly, had his department well organized and summoned his subordinates to regular after-school meetings if some communication had to be passed on and required "discussion," a term which normally implied a soliloquy on Naithsmith's part, with any attempt at reasonable suggestions peremptorily dismissed as irrelevant or nonsensical, or both. Such gatherings were also held prior to terminal class exams, when setters and correctors for the various papers were announced. When after a few years Candlish had acquired detailed knowledge of SCE standards by perusing past external papers and applied marking schemes, and was himself preparing senior pupils for both High and Lower French and German, he became more and more irritated by the unrealistically difficult and too severely marked "dummy-runs" which took place each December or January. In these tests the cream obtained only moderate marks while those less talented, but still capable, were classified as bad to abysmal, and no account was taken of the additional knowledge to be accrued and the additional practise to be had between then and the real thing in March and April (changed to April and May in 1962). This iniquitous system denied presentation many weeks later to those who had gained less than 50%; and these destructive factors, applied as they were in such a ruthless combination, amounted to no less than a travesty of educational justice. With their hearts set on a chosen career, such pupils lacked the qualifications necessary for university entrance (which was achieved by similarly endowed youngsters in other secondary schools conducted under a more benevolent régime and no doubt under the same circumstances many of them subjected to the Naithsmith yoke would also have attained their goal). Small wonder that hardly any of those presented (unless they were feeling really out of sorts) ever failed. Candlish pleaded time and time again with his Principal to reverse his decision on certain pupils but rarely convinced him he was not being emotional rather than rational. The man was not for turning.

One typical example of Naithsmith's intransigence arose over Candlish's marking of a Preliminary essay in Higher German. The possible mark was 25, and the content was so relevant and so well thought out, and the language itself of such a remarkable standard for a pupil of 17 (with only one or two minor errors) that Candlish had awarded it 23.

This was met with an explosion of derision:
"You can't do that!" fumed Naithsmith. "No pupil's essay can be worth that. Mark it down to 18."
"18?"
"Yes, 18."

Candlish felt this was neither realistic nor just.

"But this boy is the most highly gifted linguistically that I have ever had, or suspect I ever shall. He even keeps me on my toes. It's a marvellous essay."

"That means nothing. On principle you don't give anyone 23 out of 25. You'll just swell his head and make him overconfident. It's just not done."

Candlish couldn't restrain himself.

"My God, man, this pupil will be better than you or I some day. Let's give credit where it's due."

Naithsmith didn't like that, neither the language used nor what it conveyed:

"Such remarks border on insubordination. I said 18. Don't argue. I set the standards here. Subject closed."

Candlish fervently hoped that it would not be too long before he, as a Principal Teacher himself, would be in a position to set altogether different standards.

The pupil in question was to gain First Class Honours in German Language and Literature at Edinburgh and ultimately to become Professor at a southern university. Candlish hoped his ex-pupil would be more appreciative of his students' performances than Naithsmith had been of his. *

Unfortunately, and sadly, Naithsmith was not the only Principal Teacher at Abergarvie more concerned with his Department's, and therefore his own, percentage of passes than the pupils' future careers; those were men who regarded all failures, no matter how few of them there were, as ugly blots which had no right to appear on their personal copy-books. The Heads of Physics and

---

* Not long after this episode occurred the SCE Examination Board laid down the sensible and long-overdue guide line that any essay, whether at Ordinary or Higher grade or Sixth Year Studies should, if judged to be as good as could reasonably be expected at the level in question, be granted full marks. (Candlish, by then free of Naismith's clutches, learned that his former Principal heartily disapproved of the new ruling and refused to comply).

Mathematics were cut in the same selfish mould and, as we shall soon see, Candlish was to have a bitter fight on his hands when his own son reached the Fourth and Fifth years and his choice of vocation came very near to being irrevocably unrealised.

Apart from Candlish's aversion to Naithsmith's proclivity for cutting pupils and assistants alike down to size and to the man's aloof attitude to his staff, as if he were some sort of pedagogically efficient Adonis without equal anywhere, he was in the main left to his own devices and well satisfied with what he was achieving. What he found it difficult to accept was the assumed willingness of staff to run about a school football field on a Saturday morning (if not too pot-bellied to manage it) with a whistle in their mouths (if not too breathless to blow it), or to go through the painful motions of "umpiring" a cricket match on a cold, early summer evening; or to supervise noisy school lunches after a morning's hard teaching and have their ears ringing with the continual clatter of cutlery and strident voices; or to sell tickets at the main Academy door for the Music Festival or for a performance of the school play, all trivial and status-lowering pursuits which any appointed dog's body could have, and should have, performed. Status? How could they have any? Most teachers could have challenged — and beaten — the longest-necked ostriches in creation. They couldn't even see why they were held by the public at large in such low regard, and if they did see it they were quite unprepared to improve their image by standing up for themselves and telling their exploiters where they should go. It riled Candlish when potential university students, bent on becoming lawyers or doctors or engineers, told him that if they did not succeed in gaining admission to the faculty of their choice they "could always teach"; something of an ill-considered remark when made to a serving teacher, to be sure, but frank, and so indicative of the thoughts of those who observed daily what was going on. They looked on such a job as a last resort, as an uninviting but possibly wise insurance policy if their more ambitious aspirations came to nothing: they did not fancy it, they would never become rich, but they would at least be certain of their daily crust until they reached their dotage.

Not astonishing then that school teachers, especially those of the right blend, were in short supply, and in shorter and shorter supply and compelled to carry an ever weightier workload as the situation deteriorated and in some secondaries became almost untenable. And it was allowed to become thus because collectively they didn't have the guts of a louse, not even of a dead one. French teachers "taught" Maths, Maths teachers "taught" French, and Physical Education teachers "taught" everything. Yet in industry the union bosses were out there, swinging their claymores if it came to their notice that a plumber had dared to ram home a nail or a joiner to tighten a tap.

Candlish also became convinced that teaching, by its very nature, had the propensity to attract a special sort of individual: the type who is a born plitterer and would much rather engage in the aforementioned frivolous activities and inconsequential chit-chat with his charges than get down to the nitty-gritties of classroom instruction; the type to whom the four walls provide a haven in whose private confines he can be very much left to his own devices, often with no boss hanging over him, with no possibility of making crucial mistakes that would be immediately obvious in other fields and would end in severe chastisement or dismissal. Steady and safe — and no sweat.

As the staffing situation became progressively worse in the middle sixties and early seventies — even in solid foundations such as Abergarvie Academy with more likelihood of attracting beginners than the big city schools or junior secondaries like Abergarvie High — all sorts of ploys were conjured up by the Scottish Education Department in an effort to stem the rot.

Stem the rot? The geniuses esconsed in their impenetrable strongholds in Edinburgh would have been awarded few marks for far-sightedness, or for elementary sanitation, believing as they did that you stemmed the rot by helping it to spread into every corner of the woodwork. The curtain was about to go up on a comedy of Monty Pythonesque proportions... considered by its authors to be a brilliant and original innovation to make more promising the promotion prospects of experienced and frustrated Assistant Teachers, even the best of whom were condemned to a period of as much as 15 years without a morale-boosting lift to the status of Principal Teacher, was the creation of the post of "Special Assistant", ostensibly to reward those who habitually presented candidates for the SCE, with all the preparation and correction which that entailed, but frequently used to keep staff where they were and to attract others from outwith the county areas. In a largish school with a teaching complement of around 60, perhaps 10 or 12 of these carrots would be offered — and eagerly grasped as some sort of compensation for their efforts. The award amounted initially to £55 per annum. Not much, even then, but many deserving of it didn't get it and some got it who didn't deserve it. The latter were invariably lured from other authorities.

Allied to this was yet another brainchild concocted by these same faceless boffins hidden away in the backrooms of St Andrews House — the serious and, they thought, laudable suggestion that teachers of Maths and Science — where the shortages were most acute — should be paid more than their equivalently qualified colleagues in other subjects. Once again they lacked the foresight — not that much foresight was required — to realise that such a recipe contained even more ingredients for individual and inter-departmental jealousies and ill-feeling. It had to be pointed out that for one thing if for no other, such a desperate and deplorable trick could — and would — result in a complete nincompoop "teaching" Maths earning more than a highly competent colleague next door whose subject was English or History. Hornets' nests were already there aplenty and for once Scottish teachers were sufficiently incensed and sufficiently determined to have the scheme abandoned before it got off the ground. But the fact that it was even mooted tells more than a little about those who were running the country's education system.

But worse, far worse, was to come, and to keep on coming. When one member of Naithsmith's staff decided to get married and move to Aberdeen, no-one applied for the vacancy. Candlish was now the father of a second child and in order to make some extra money he had taken on a weekly evening class, and was asked by Naithsmith — he who would not tolerate ineptitude in his department — whether any of his adult students had sufficient knowledge of French to handle First Year classes. When Candlish expressed his surprise at the request — and made no attempt to camouflage his disgust — Naithsmith tried to justify his action by stating that if no-one could be found the existing staff would become more burdened than ever and forego some of their non-teaching time, of which there was little enough to start with.

No, Candlish answered, he couldn't think of anyone, and even if the reverse had been the case his response would have been exactly the same. Then, still shocked that a Head of Department should advocate such a step, he added:

"I've got to say it — I'm flabbergasted. Surely resorting to such measures only degrades us further and helps to perpetuate the whole rotten situation. In the event of a scarcity of doctors, for instance, can you imagine someone with a rudimentary knowledge of first-aid or nappy rash being welcomed into the medical profession? What would be the reaction of qualified doctors? Of the BMA? Of the public? It's outrageous."

"Well, as I've pointed out, it means more work for us if we can't get someone."

Candlish, needless to say, did not get someone, but Naithsmith did — a geriatric whose total knowledge of the language derived from the breaks he had had from the trenches during the First World War. Mind you, he had been back in France on a couple of short visits since then.

Unfortunately the teachers themselves and their representative bodies, being made of much more anaemic stuff than the medics and their BMA, just stood aside and took all this; and took it so much that in many schools it virtually became the norm.

Another dilutive measure, designed to cope with the increasing scarcity of primary teachers, recruited more girls into that sphere of education by lowering the entrance qualifications to Moray House or Jordanhill from two Highers and three Lowers to — wait for it — one Higher and a *near miss* on the other. No dairyman dared water his milk to that extent. The Civil Servants had become gamblers who doubled their stakes on every losing throw. And we all know where that leads.

A further ploy was the recruitment of tradesmen such as joiners and metal-workers who, after brief attendance at a Training College, became fully-fledged "teachers" and were let loose on the schools. They were often, as might be expected, highly inarticulate, spoke a thoroughly bastardized form of "English" and found it difficult to open their mouths without indulging in the superfluous expletives normally heard in abundance on the worksites whence they had come. Yet strange enough — or perhaps on reflection it was not strange at all — they seemed better suited to tame the tough nuts in their classes than other instructors whose language was more civilized; no doubt they were better understood and regarded as more kindred spirits. One of them, whom Candlish knew, was at least aware of his intellectual inadequacies and shied away from all staffroom contact to spend each lunch-hour sitting on a toilet-seat with his *Daily Record.*

With so many tragi-comic acts being concocted in the administrative loony-bin it is difficult to say which of them ranked as the most tragic — or comic — of the lot; but the brazen gambit which went under the title of "Designated Schools" and was introduced when staff shortages were making some schools unmanageable, must have occupied a high position on this list.

A school qualified for "designation" if its required staffing complement fell below a certain level. As compensation for the extra work load an additional payment of £200 per annum was made to each member of staff, plus travelling expenses to those who lived a minimum distance from the town. So what happened? Footloose youngsters, who were ready to grasp at every penny they could get, and some, who would never be young again but still grasped at every penny, seized their chance and moved from a non-designated school to one that had become designated. The result of such a brainwave should have been foreseen, but no! Schools that had been labelled "designated" almost immediately got an influx of new bodies (thanks to adverts in the national press, which were presented in such a way as to suggest that those appointed would be joining some sort of educational El Dorado) and soon became undesignated; and of course the reverse happened when the institutions from which they had poured became themselves designated; staffing levels in individual schools rose and fell like well-oiled yo-yos; out, in , in, out; faces changed as in a transit camp and timetables changed with the frequency of traffic lights. Yet you had to laugh, even if the laughter was of the hysterical kind, because in what ought to have been the unlikeliest of settings both teachers and pupils were pitched headlong into what could only be described as a novel version of musical chairs. Or, rather, very unmusical chairs.

As more and more patches were slapped over the ever-widening cracks and the material used was the shabbiest that could be found, Candlish and those equally demoralised knew that the profession's only means of salvation lay in the formation of one strong, united union, not two or three playing into the politicians' hands with their silly internecine squabbles, and with a leader cast in the real militant mould. But they couldn't imagine that ever happening: too many petty loyalties to too many ineffectual bodies for them to extricate themselves from the morass in which they wallowed so pitifully.

Why did teachers themselves and the general public, in an educationally aware country such as Scotland, accept all the makeshift and self-destructive absurdities outlined above? True, a willingness to accept — which in this case is no more than a euphemism for a chronic lack of mettle — is a characteristic of the teaching profession as a near whole, but why the general reluctance on the part of thinking parents to go well beyond merely complaining amongst themselves and to demand with one resolute and unequivocal voice that the necessary steps be taken to end a situation that had rapidly become no less than farcical and belonged to the realms of the incredible?

We are dealing only with education, of course, not with a matter of life and death. Yet perhaps, like the game of football as it was once described by one of its best known managers, it should be considered more important than that.

* * *

Yet teaching did have its less serious moments — admittedly not too many — and when these did occur they were welcomed as soul-saving little interludes amid the daily turmoil. One morning, while Candlish was standing outside his classroom door supervising the orderly movement of bodies along the corridor during a change of period (a duty rarely insisted upon nowadays) a sixth-former came up to him and said:

"Excuse me, sir. Miss Brown wants to know if she can come and have a word with you at 4 o'clock?"

"Miss Brown? Who on earth is she?"

"You know, Miss Brown the Maths teacher, sir."

"Brown? But there's no Miss Brown in the Maths Department!"

The boy suddenly looked abashed and his face reddened:
"Oh, I'm sorry, sir. I mean Miss Jefferson."

Explanation: at a distance of two feet anyone would have taken Miss Jefferson for a certain member of the Broon family in the *Sunday Post* comic and on her very first day in the school had been christened "Daphne" by the pupils. Hence Miss "Brown".

Chapter 4
THE "INTERVIEW"

After some ten years as an Assistant Teacher (latterly as a Special Assistant), Candlish was eager to free himself of Naithsmith's shackles and to acquire a department of his own — not by any means an easy task because, as we have already mentioned, such posts were few and far between and attracted hordes of applicants. Naithsmith had told him — and he appreciated his action since no-one wanted to lose an experienced and competent member of staff — that he considered him now quite capable of filling such a position and that he ought to apply for any he saw advertised in the quality Scottish press, which meant in "The Scotsman" or "The Glasgow Herald" (the "Glasgow" had not yet been dropped) or in the weekly journal published by the Educational Institute of Scotland.

Candlish was interviewed, unsuccessfully, for two, which had entailed journeys to Aberdeen and Ayr; and suspected, rightly, that both of them had been all sewn up beforehand. He was rushed through one or two questions, with no-one paying much attention to his answers, but then all the legal motions had to be observed, even if this incurred needless expenditure on travelling and possibly overnight accommodation on the part of the interviewing authority and equally needless disruption of Candlish's classes and his colleagues' timetables during his absence.

Then another chance. The school was in Glentilloch, a town somewhat smaller than Abergarvie, only 15 miles distant and whose junior secondary had just been upgraded to senior secondary (previously Fourth Year pupils upwards had made the daily journey to Abergarvie). This time Candlish did what he knew he should not have been required to do, what he did not really want to do or ought to do, but which he knew he had to do because there were few who did not do it — and apparently did so to their advantage: a bit of canvassing amongst those who would be present for the appointment and whose word counted for something in the neighbourhood. It did not take him long to get round them.

The interview took place before the entire committee of the County Council, whose members consisted of men — no women — ranging from a minister of religion and a gin-soaked landowner to butchers and bakers — literally — and perhaps including the odd candlestick-maker as well. The Director of Education introduced Candlish and referred amongst other things to his very fine war record, at which point a grossly overweight butcher, for whom the recent world upheaval had hardly existed as far as any personal discomfort was concerned, somewhat rudely interrupted him by asking why such a fact should be considered important. The war was always a touchy point with him and he was known locally for having made a fortune out of under-counter dealings, while the only blood he had seen was that which dripped from the carcasses hanging in his shop. For him life was centred totally on the size of bullocks — or bollocks, especially his own. Yet he rated himself highly as a public speaker by dint of his daily sessions of tittle-tattle with his women customers. And he had more ammunition in his belt:

"I see frae this sheet that the applicant has a Hon ... an Honours Degree in French an' German. But diz he hae his Highers?" (Someone had once told him of their existence and he made the most of this titbit of knowledge at every opportunity).

The Director coughed then looked towards the Reverend Hugh McCall:

"Mr McCall, do you have any questions you wish to put to Mr Candlish?" A bit superfluous, really, because any minister present, and there was always a minister present, always had a question he wanted to put to the applicant, whoever it was. It was always the same question.

Candlish expected it. He already knew of the rôle played by the Church on such occasions:

"Mr Candlish, you certainly have a very fine war record behind you — not that I approve of what our bombers did to Germany, mind you — and by all accounts you are an excellent language teacher, but tell me, are you prepared to take classes in Religious Instruction? Just as important in our view you know!"

In *our* view! What the hell had *they* to do with it?

Candlish wanted to say that he thought he was being interviewed for the post of Principal Teacher of modern Languages, but was well aware that such a remark would in no way improve his chances; he had been advised by some of those who had gone this way before that these would be much reduced if he failed to give the right answer, and that they would be reduced to nil if another applicant stated he was willing to take on the post of part-time preacher into the bargain. The great majority of interviewees had no intention of fulfilling such a pledge and, if appointed, would use the allotted time to catch up on correction or preparation whilst the pupils did their homework for the following day or read books. But by the law of the land RI had to appear on the curriculum, and appearing on the curriculum was usually as far as it got.

"Yes."

The Reverend Hugh McCall smiled his satisfaction. The Moderator would have approved of his performance.

Came the turn of Mr Bert Sinclair, vaguely aware of his own intellectual inadequacies and who knew or had seen little of this world apart from the insides of his vast tomato greenhouses and his collection of plastic gnomes, of which he had more in his exposed garden than he had books in his house. So the brightly painted figures stood there in massed array as irrefutable testimony to his love of art in one of its most exquisite forms.

"Wull ye tak' pairt in some o' thae extra curr... curric... curriculier activities?"

Once more there could be only one answer:

"Yes."

"Whut yins?"

Candlish could force himself to be diplomatic only up to a certain point:

"Flying lessons?"

But he smiled benignly as he uttered the words. Only the Director laughed good-humouredly. Some looked in Candlish's direction and raised their eyebrows; some just stared into space or at the table in front of them; others wondered where the aircraft would come from. And what about an airfield? You needed an airfield; maybe Scone — that wasn't too far away.

The Director broke the awkward silence:

"Any more questions, gentlemen?"

No more questions. After all, it was somewhat risky to venture beyond the usual stereotyped query, especially with this fellow; you could make a fool of yourself, although admittedly most members of the interviewing committee didn't even know when they were doing that.

"Good. Then I think we should get Mr Candlish over to Glentilloch as soon as possible. All agreed?"

One or two nodded their heads. Some glanced at their watches. The butcher grunted.

Candlish rose, looked at the Director, said "Thank you" and walked out of the chamber, wondering just how much importance was attached to the position of Principal Teacher. And to other things.

Such thoughts appeared to be confirmed in graphic fashion while he chatted to an acquaintance outside the main door and saw his butcher friend make the most of climbing aboard his big personalized Mercedes, Registration No. BUL 1. The same palaver was affected by the tomato-grower with his black and gold wheels and his battery of headlights. But his was a mere BMW.

Chapter 5
COMPREHENSIVE *EDIFICATION*

Candlish arrived at Glentilloch to take over a so-called Department of Modern Languages which, practically speaking, existed so far in name only since the school, as already stated, had just been upgraded to senior secondary status; and it would therefore take some time for classes to gradually build up to Sixth Year and for other subjects, such as an additional foreign language (German) to be introduced. Up till then a single teacher of French, who seemed to be overawed at the prospect of eventually presenting candidates for an external examination, was all that had been required.

The contrast with Abergarvie could hardly have been more marked. Whereas the latter, a highly selective school, had boasted very large complements in IV, V and VI, it was obvious to Candlish from the outset that such a desirable situation would never develop at Glentilloch, which was now to cater for all secondary pupils within a radius of 10 miles.

The general standards of speech, demeanour and dress of the new pupils contrasted vividly — all too vividly — with those of his former charges in Abergarvie, reflecting the fact that the area was predominantly agricultural and its inhabitants less affluent; yet there were, as there always are, even in the most downtrodden surroundings, a few youngsters of superior intelligence, mainly the offspring of the handful of professional parents who lived in or around the town, but also a smattering from backgrounds which could hardly have been described as beneficial as far as heredity or scholastic encouragement were concerned. But, thankfully, rare specks of gold are, in this sphere at any rate, nearly always to be found amongst the piles of dross.

What shocked him right away was the poor grasp of the language shown by pupils at each stage; their teacher of several years standing (he had taught nowhere else) was an affable and lively enough individual but he had been left to his own devices and had no idea of the discipline required to prepare pupils for the SCE. That was the trouble with staff who in their isolated backwaters found themselves, without even realising it, away off track in more senses than one. Candlish told him, and others of little experience who arrived as the school roll (and its rôle) grew, to peruse recent French "O" Grade papers and to familiarize themselves with the type of content, standard of language, breadth of vocabulary, length of questions and so on and so forth, stressing that half the battle in successful presentation was a thorough awareness of how examiners' minds worked; no valuable time and effort to be wasted on material which was away off beam or superfluous. Although this might appear to be a simple procedure to follow Candlish never failed to find it amazing that so many intelligent people just could not come to terms with it; they lacked the knack, or the self-discipline, or whatever it was.

After a few years, with Classes IV to VI fully established, with German on the curriculum, and with more pupils tending to stay on at school, the Department consisted of four full-time and one part-time staff (the latter a lady who agreed to come in to teach some German but only if she had the final period of both morning and afternoon sessions off each day so that she could attend to more important activities such as her shopping). It annoyed Candlish that the Rector accepted her on such conditions; her First Year university German was away under par in any case, and her accent truly abominable, but happily she was soon shown the door when a fully qualified young man, albeit a beginner, was appointed. For some considerable time Candlish found himself teaching teachers almost as much as he was teaching pupils, but he gradually knocked the Department into reasonable shape and was quite satisfied with its progress. He was looked upon as a taskmaster, but a taskmaster who was always helpful and scrupulously fair.

Then it happened.

It came under the name of Comprehensive Education.

* * *

For over two thousand years classes had been organised on the principle — and in all that time no-one had suggested there might be a better way — that the smaller the spread of intellect in any single teaching group the more efficient the teaching and the easier it was for both teachers and taught. You concentrated on those occupying the middle rung on the ladder of ability so that the difficulties experienced by those below it, and the frustrations of those above it, were kept to a minimum; the gifted did not become too bored and the less endowed could normally survive if given a little extra help and encouragement. However a momentous discovery had just been made: we'd been getting it all bloody wrong since Plato was a lad.

Up till about 1974, by which time the new system had been almost universally adopted in Scotland, only two First Year classes at Glentilloch High School (which we shall take as a typical example) had begun to study the French language, the other eight having been considered incapable of making any headway in what was for them too demanding a subject. But not any longer: the streamed designations IA and 1B disappeared overnight and the nomenclature for the new entrants became 1B, 1D, !F, 1H, 1K, 1M, 1P, 1S, 1V and 1X, each with 31 or 32 pupils. All very democratic; no more of the former stigmatising grading as they were now all sorted out alphabetically. 1B was made up of those whose surnames began with A to C, while 1D accommodated D to F, and so on. "Mixed Ability Classes" was the operative term. And it was some mixture: a lunatic pot-pourri in which potential Honours Graduates rubbed shoulders with potential lavatory attendants. Yes, the light that heralded equal educational opportunity for all had at last been switched on, and with such dazzling power that it blinded all those who had to try to come to terms with a régime so farcical and so painfully comic at times that it could have been trumped up by only the most offbeat of minds. Moreover it was largely irrelevant in Scotland in the political sense because in Scotland, by time-honoured tradition, poor but academically gifted children had never been denied their chance. The sole aristocracy in matters educational had always been one of intellect. So ironic it was that the same aristocracy were now to be imperilled in their studies by the too close proximity of the unintellectual masses.

As far as French was concerned, all ten First Years at Glentilloch were to follow the same audio-visual course, one of the many which had suddenly spawned like asphyxiating fungi and were masterpieces of boring, repetitive simplicity. Candlish chose the one he considered the least objectionable of a thoroughly uninspiring bunch, which hardly constituted a recommendation for any of the others. Yet this was one of the newfangled "open sesames" which immediately sold in their tens and tens of thousands thanks to the gigantic increase — something in the nature of 500% — in the number of pupils now let loose on the language (not an inappropriate phrase, as we shall shortly see). Alert educational authors and publishers and tape recorder manufacturers, who had seen what was afoot and had prepared themselves accordingly, rubbed their hands bare in unconcealed glee, whilst those who harboured Candlish's fears did the opposite and wrung theirs: bulging pockets for a few, empty heads or mental torture for the many. The old maxim about an ill wind retained its full validity.

The subject matter and exercises in the course reluctantly selected by Candlish were tedious, stereotyped, and, for those with above average IQs, so simple and stultifying as to defy belief. Any new syntax or vocabulary the author had dared to introduce in each lesson was so scant as to be difficult to find, and in the questions to be answered by the pupils there was such wholesale repetition that everyone, teachers included, was made dizzy trying to see how each differed from the one, or ones, which preceded it (normally only a single word or the word order was changed); grammatical rules were totally ignored and unexplained, the implication being that they were artificial and to be avoided; "*je vais*" would be followed later in the text by "*nous allons*", but that was nothing to wonder or worry about: irregular verbs didn't exist as such — you just picked them up effortlessly and subconsciously as you went along. No need for such ordeals as having to learn them off in their dozens. You learned French the natural way, the way French children learned it, by listening and imitating. Pity this godsent method failed to recognise the all-important fact, which will just not go away, that unlike French juveniles, foreign students of their language had another to contend with — their own — which they had already been speaking for several years and was their means of communication for all but some 30 or 40 minutes of each day. True, the principle of *laissez faire,* now applied to modern language teaching, might have swept away many of the crippling inhibitions created in pupils by the traditional approach, but this revolutionary alternative, emphasising oral proficiency, merely offered a hotchpotch of parrot calls because the knowledge of vocabulary and grammar required for coherent speech was conspicuously lacking. So a marked improvement in speaking ability, at last being rightly stressed as the most valuable asset for the majority of pupils (and which made a modern language to all intents and purposes a practical subject requiring small groups) did not materialise. But how could it? And in any case how could a teacher aspire to effective oral work in the space of little more than half-an-hour each day and confronted with a class of 30 or more? All he can do is go through the motions. Theory and practice. In this sphere at any rate never the twain shall meet. At least under the old system able pupils could read literature in the foreign language and write in it commendably well. No, they couldn't speak it, but now they speak it no better — and reading and writing have gone overboard.

And the result of the availability of French to almost all and sundry took the form of a complete reversal of the pundits' predictions: the poor wee buggers who had so long been educationally — and criminally — neglected and who were now at long last studying a foreign language were made more conscious than ever of their own inadequacies as they made feeble attempts to learn something and were shown up in mixed ability classes by the more talented. At least in the past they had all been in the same midden; but now, in no time at all, they detested a subject which far outstripped their intellectual capabilities; they found it beyond them to repeat a single word with any degree of accuracy after a dozen attempts. You got the usual dolts, of course, who just sat their like zombies, at first unperturbed, then eternally fidgeting and often becoming disruptive, but every group also contained those of a more sensitive nature who soon became distressingly aware of their impotence, scared stiff they would be asked a question, scared stiff the brighter elements would laugh and scoff and jeer as they clumsily blurted out absurd answers or just sat and stared at the floor and squirmed. Candlish did not feel sorry only for himself, and soon decided to save such youngsters embarrassment, and the more receptive invaluable time, by concentrating solely on the latter. It was the best policy for all concerned, but one which, had it become known, would have been more than frowned upon — in fact severely repudiated — by those who knew best. He would have been denounced as a traitor to the cause. But to hell with those who had visited this upon them.

It is true that, in view of the special difficulties inherent in trying to teach French to pupils of low intelligence, modern language teachers — for whom this was both a novel and a galling experience — were undoubtedly more adversely affected than colleagues concerned with other disciplines. Up till now they had known only the high-fliers and some who did not fly quite so high but were still teachable. But this is not intended to suggest that those responsible for other subjects of study did not also have their problems: although History and Geography, for instance, could to a certain extent be presented pictorially or in story form, the same sort of treatment was seldom possible in Mathematics or the Sciences; and as for a foreign language, it is there as it exists and cannot be simplified.

Forecasting the outcome of such an upheaval was hardly a formidable task; in a word, the welfare and the future prospects of an able minority were to be willingly sacrificed for, at best, a highly unlikely benefit to an academically inconsequential majority. Every last vestige of a vile and socially unacceptable system of segregation was to be swept away in one gigantic swoop. Never in the long history of pedagogy was so much to be suffered by so many for the good of no-one at all. *The cream was to be shamelessly curdled to coddle the clots.*

And that was by no means all. The sure, steady course that had been successfully steered during all those centuries was to undergo a radical change demanding vast expenditure, not only on resources, but on hundreds of extra teachers at a time when many schools were already operating ineffectively because teachers were so thin on the classroom floor. Although the folly of all this was pointed out vociferously — and, because the complainants were the teachers themselves, beggingly — the authors of the scheme did not want to know. The storm would blow over, as it always did, for teachers "were a conscientious lot, devoted to their noble profession, and would always cope". Of course they would. They would put up with anything. That's why education was in such a mess.

By no means the least galling factor was the blatant hypocrisy of those who strutted around wearing their correct political hat and paid lip service to their masters. A typical example was that of one of Her Majesty's District Inspectors, who went the rounds of the authority's schools drooling at the mouth as he extolled the unimaginable virtues of the great new concept and expressing his heartfelt regret that not everyone seemed to share his views. Strange then that with the implementation of the system in the state school attended by his two sons (Abergarvie Academy), Jeremy and Jason were whisked off to a private institution in Edinburgh; and many other professed socialists, including notable figures such as Shirley Williams, did likewise — and, decades later, by which time the resultant fruits appeared to be even poorer apologies for what had been promised, she was joined in her defection by Labour leader Tony Blair, then by Harriet Harman; an admission that the new system had failed in its twin aims: to produce the desired results in the classroom and to create a more egalitarian society. As for the second of these, it was obvious to all and sundry that the gap was steadily widening between those who had much and those who had little.

But to return to the early 70s. No support for the antis from the "prestigious" (the epithet is its own) Educational Institute of Scotland either, an organization which prided itself on being the solid foundation stone — and, incredibly, the sharp-eyed watchdog of Scottish education; nor from the Scottish Secondary Teachers' Association (a "rebel" body formed in 1947 supposedly to combat the policy of the primary teacher orientated EIS but eschewed by many whose allegiance it should have gained but didn't because of surprising wishy-washiness on its part or apathy on their own). These two institutions remained true to form as they bleated out their timorous objections (usually prefaced by an unctuous "with due respect") to established authority concerning the unworkability of the new code in the difficult circumstances that prevailed — and exerted about as much clout as the proverbial feather duster. As always they were afraid to say "boo" to the fat geese in their comfortable pens in Edinburgh, far removed from the increasing number of traumas endured by those in the front line (and of course some of their senior officials cultivated political ambitions, a job for which they seemed to be eminently suited). Further, in the ranks of the teachers themselves there were many who acquiesced and refused to add their weight to the protests and the threats of more spunky colleagues and whose nature was to kowtow at every opportunity to those they considered to be their superiors. We could observe some sense of propriety by saying they were unabashed sycophants who made even the mildest of the protesters blush, but, on reflection, such a description would be a gross understatement of the true facts: the extent of their obsequiousness was such that they were prepared to lick more than mere feet — and did so regularly.

There was a third teachers' "union", the small Scottish Schoolmasters Association, formed in 1933 and regarded by all outside it as being "militant", which to be sure is a relative term, depending on the context in which you are operating. Mere threats to discontinue such abominations as playground supervision during the lunch-hour hardly constituted bold and decisive action. Militant? The miners and the car-workers would have laughed their heads off and said the teachers did not know what the word meant. But at least, and taking into account the paucity of its members (it was well nigh a stigma to be one) the SSA generally displayed far more drive and guts than either the EIS or the SSTA. Its *raison d'etre* stemmed from the conviction that male teachers were held back in their quest for higher salaries by the presence of so many women, especially those of the married kind, who were well enough off financially and therefore cared little about their male counterparts' demands, and gave them little support, if any at all. But the SSA seemed fated to remain a fringe organization and never attained the backing it deserved. In 1968 it somewhat enigmatically decided to admit females and in 1975 it amalgamated with the obscure Women Teachers' Association and in 1980 changed its name to the ponderous-sounding National Association of Schoolmasters/Union of Women Teachers (NASUWT).

In 1968 and 1969 the EIS and the SSTA expressed both surprise and horror — or so they made out — when some of their more exasperated and less submissive members began to propose, as the SSA had already done, the desirability of strike action. Strike action? Were they hearing right? Uttering the very word was nothing short of blasphemy. Teachers going on strike? Lowering themselves to the level of the Bolshie workers in the factories and the miners down the pits? When it was pointed out to them that the workers in the factories and the miners down the pits often enjoyed a higher standard of living than they did (and often with little by way of hard-earned qualifications), that cut no ice either. "Think of the children!" was their perpetual line of defence — a cry fiercely and mockingly dismissed as sanctimonious balderdash by all those who had become both weary of and angry at their unions' unwillingness to do something positive, and who stressed again and again that it was precisely because they were "thinking of the children" that they believed that the time had come to resort to the only means left to them. You didn't educate children effectively, they insisted, in classes of up to 50 pupils and by alienating promising recruits to the profession by offering them financial peanuts. This was the second half of the 20th Century and gone for ever was the erstwhile image of the ascetic schoolmaster content with his books and untroubled by his impecuniousness. In modern living teachers needed money like everyone else. Nor did you increase educational opportunity by raising the statutory leaving age at a most inopportune moment and at the same time by treating all pupils as intellectual equals, as if all you needed to do with those at the foot of the heap was place them on school benches and knowledge would automatically come flooding up through their bottoms. No, the patchwork quilt could take no more patches. Every means had been tried, many of which had lowered even further what had remained of professional prestige, and the only remedy was a substantial rise in salaries. That was the all-important panacea which would have the twofold effect of pulling in young graduates who were being attracted elsewhere by the lure of much juicier plums and of raising the low status of teachers in the eyes of the public. In our materialistic society, unfortunately, a person's worth is too often judged by how much he earns and not by how he earns it. That is the reason why people nowadays have much more respect for the skilled industrial worker or the bobby on the beat — or in a panda. The quality car in the drive and exotic foreign holidays are the modern criteria of success; a high degree of literacy does not, in the eyes of many, matter a damn. Very sad, but also very true. It was also very sad that the EIS and the SSTA stubbornly refused to entertain such arguments. Upholding the dignity of the profession was what mattered most. No comment necessary.

  To provide an opportunity for members of the different associations (and for those who would have nothing to do with any of them) to air their views, staff meetings were held in schools all over the place. The Rector of Glentilloch called his own.

  Roughly 65% of the teachers present belonged to the EIS, 25% to the SSTA, and 5% to the SSA. The remainder owed allegiance to none of these, and in reply to those who accused them of reaping the rewards of the unions' efforts without joining their ranks, the non-members retorted that any improvements in salary or working conditions were not gained thanks to these bodies, but in spite of them. They would be quite happy, they said, to support one which carried the weight of the BMA or the NUM, and to pay a substantial sum for the privilege; but they had no intention of setting their seal of approval, which membership would suggest, on a bunch of spineless toadies who, when in their most bellicose mood, produced at best a few barely audible rattles from their wooden sabres. Get them something with the sharp teeth of a shark rather than the soft gums of a codfish and they would sign up right away.

The meeting opened with the school representatives, first of the EIS and then of the SSTA, outlining the situation as their respective organizations saw it, and the plans they had to bring about improvement (at least they admitted that there was room for that). Of course they would continue to "negotiate" in a way that befitted the profession. That was splendid news for a start. News? The usual lacklustre stuff was spewed forth in ever thickening draughts of hot air. You would have witnessed more drive and decisiveness at a meeting of the Ladies' Rural called to arrange a date for their next whist drive.

Then the SSA man, relegated to the last position in the spouting order, rose to his feet, his bellicose expression heightened by his shock of red hair. Tom McEwan was a teacher of Modern Studies with a thorough knowledge of the history of Trade Unionism and of all it had achieved. Not surprising, therefore, that in contrast to the hens which had just finished their cackling he came over like a raging bull in full charge:

"I'm going to be straight. I'm sick to my fingertips of all this conciliatory, mealy-mouthed talk. It makes me — and I mean this — ashamed to belong to such a yellow-bellied lot of individuals as you. All the EIS and SSTA ever do is belch forth never-ending streams of — I'll be polite — unadulterated claptrap. And look where it has got us — absolutely nowhere, except firmly in the pockets of the mandarins who call the tune. What we need is concerted action — and now. None of us need have any scruples about adopting the only means left to us. For once, for God's sake, let's present a united front. Wrangling amongst ourselves on matters of real consequence such as new salary scales and improved conditions simply plays into the hands of the politicians by enabling them to say, quite rightly, that we ourselves don't know what we want. So let's stop argy-bargying like old fishwives and do something positive.

As you perhaps know, the SSA is planning to do just that and we would like the EIS and the SSTA to join us for purposes of solidarity. If we all act in a really determined manner and stick to our guns we can beat them. Only by doing so will we get somewhere. It is obvious by now that strike action is the only answer."

"Strike action?" screamed a woman hysterically from the body of the hall. "Strike action? I did not think I would ever live to see the day when a member of the teaching profession would ever make such an obscene suggestion. I for one would *never, never"* — so emphatically did she enunciate the negative particle that an unladylike jet of saliva shot forth for all to see — "contemplate such a degrading step. No, not under any circumstances. For one thing I am far too concerned with the welfare of the children."

Candlish stood up:

"Very original, Mrs Banks. Some of us are somewhat weary of listening to that self-righteous gibberish. If you were really concerned with the welfare of the pupils — and the welfare of the teaching staff, many of whom are young married men with children who are finding it very hard to maintain a decent standard of living — then you would not — and I make no apologies for saying it — spit out (appreciative laughter) such undiluted hogwash, because that is what it is." (Mrs Banks was a childless married woman who, then in her middle fifties, had taught all her life and whose husband held an executive post with a big insurance company. Two expensive cars, expensive cruises, the lot).

"Well, if people insist on having children that is their lookout."

Candlish, not often at a loss for words, stared at her, aghast. Christ, that's what you were up against. And the woman had an Honours degree. Some grimaced, others guffawed. A few coughed out their embarrassment.

Tom McEwan got up again:

"Ladies and Gentlemen, you've just heard one of the reasons

why an increasing number of male teachers are deserting the EIS and the SSTA to join us. We men are held back at every turn because there are so many female members of the profession who use it for their own ends, and the main end is pin money. They are quite happy with their lot. I would ask all you non-members of the SSA to consider this fact because if we can increase our membership appreciably we shall be in a much stronger position and won't let up until we are paid salaries which are not geared to women and will be on a par with those of other professions. We are planning a series of one-day strikes and we have the support of all our members. We also hope to have the support of the EIS and the SSTA."

"I can't listen to any more of this," howled Mrs Banks. "You are as bad as Arthur Scargill and God forbid that we should have you and your like in the teaching profession. You should be ostracised."

"And you, madam, should be fossilized. If you're not that already."

Teachers' meetings did not normally follow such a pattern. The Rector, in his capacity as Chairman, considered it politic to intervene:

"Ladies and Gentlemen, please! This is supposed to be a civilized discussion, not a bar-room brawl. And please keep personal criticism out of it. Mr Candlish, did you raise your hand to say something else?"

"Yes, thank you. I agree entirely that strike action is, sadly, the only means left to us, and I for one am willing to quit the SSTA for the SSA as it is the only body which shows any spunk and is prepared to act. Mr McEwan is quite right in what he says about the large proportion of apathetic women — although you can't exclude all the men from that category either. But it is a fact and not an opinion — I have seen it both here and elsewhere — that far too many female teachers use the profession for their own selfish ends, especially those who are temporary, taking time off when they feel like a day's shopping in Glasgow or Edinburgh or simply because they feel like it. However I do not approve of one-day stoppages. The SSA does not have enough members — not so far at any rate — to disrupt any school without the co-operation of at least one of the other unions, but in any case what purpose is served by staying away for a single day? All you do is lose that day's pay. Even if the entire staff of a school stayed at home you would merely have council officials smile all over their faces at the thought of saving a few hundred pounds on wages. And they know that the loss of one day's lessons isn't going to harm pupils' progress very much — that is to say those who make any progress. No, let's have our strikes, but they must be designed to create widespread disruption and you won't achieve that by a single day's absence now and again."

Convulsions from Mrs Banks, and much spluttering and dark looks from those who held her views. Applause from others.

The EIS and SSTA representatives counter-attacked, if that is not too strong a term, by replaying their same scratchy old record: teachers must maintain their professional dignity and their high standing in the community. But on this occasion much of the smugness drained from their faces when their fatuous procrastinations elicited more than a few impatient "Achs" and expressions of derision from the gathering.

Candlish did not even deign to heap his scorn upon them. He continued:

"Well, let's get back to the real world. Even if you closed a school for a week or two now and again that would still have little effect. Loss of more wages, that's all. Some parents would object, but on the whole the thinking ones appreciate our position and the objectors would be mostly working mothers mainly concerned with the welfare of their offspring while they were out at work. We need to go much further than that. We..."

"But with longer strikes few of us would survive financially," interrupted a young chap at the back.

"Exactly, but allow me to finish. What we must hold is an *indefinite* strike, which would go on for ever if need be. All you need do is send out one or two respected schools, and also one or two which are not, shall we say, regarded as being in the same category. The rest of us would contribute a pound or two per week to ensure that the absent staff received their normal wages. Parents of pupils at such establishments as Bearsden Academy or Madras College — or at Clydebank High or Armadale Academy would demand: "Why us?" That would cause a real furore. Furthermore hordes of bored kids roaming the streets would get up to all sorts of mischief without the daily discipline of attending school. Remember "Lord of the Flies". It's the only feasible and effective way of doing it."

The EIS reply:

"That would be anarchy!"

"It's anarchy now."

"The EIS is determined to live up to the unqualified respect it has deservedly enjoyed nationwide, yes, even worldwide, since its inception in 1848, as the recognised body responsible for the high standing of Scottish education. I can only say that such irresponsible talk appals me. There are more dignified ways of doing things, you know." "Dignity" again. At that juncture both McEwan and Candlish emitted despairing groans, made their apologies to the Chairman and walked out. When a surprising number of others followed their lead, Candlish felt a surge of hope because, for the first time in his recollection, the sheep were not the ones who followed but the ones who stayed where they were.

In Glentilloch itself conditions plunged into the realm of the farcical when the number of teachers short, out of a required complement of 65, increased to 17. A similar situation prevailed in many other establishments, and with it the attendant ills: those who were there were worked to a frazzle covering extra classes, which led to a classic example of the catch-22 syndrome as staff became over-stressed and even ill, or took odd days off in an effort to recharge their depleted batteries. Never before had timetables been rendered so flexible — perhaps chaotic would be a better description — since they were first invented; surely never before had rectors and their deputés spent so much of their working day struggling to fit in this piece and that piece as if engaged in some sort of novel jigsaw which more often than not proved to be insoluble. On days when doubling-up of classes or herding four or five of them together in the assembly hall still failed to cater for all, only one practicable step remained: the unattended were sent home and told to stay there for the time being. This arrangement applied, need it be said, only to non-certificate and to the poorer certificate groups — not that the staff voiced any complaints on that score — and constituted a blatant denial of the recently implemented doctrine which stated unequivocally that all were equal and must have equal opportunity. Apparently when it came down to basics, pragmatism won the day. For one thing the parents of some SCE pupils might have had something to say had such exclusion been the lot of their own; not that the others remained mute — but for different reasons, as has been noted.

When exploited and demoralized teachers claimed, undeniably with much justification, that the huge sum being saved on salaries should be shared out amongst those bearing the extra burden — which at least would offer them some reward for their exhausted state — the reply was as might have been expected:

"No, good gracious no! You are being thoroughly mercenary and are breaching professional etiquette. You are supposed to be above such deliberations. Such a money-conscious attitude is totally alien to the ethos of the profession."

Teaching was always a "profession" when it suited them to say so. Behave like professionals but do not expect to be treated as such.

As the position worsened — yes, it was allowed to drop to further depths — and the number of teachers in favour of strike action outnumbered those who were not, the EIS and the SSTA were ultimately forced to bow to their members wishes in 1970 and to enter a field in which they were reluctant amateurs. The two bodies co-operated for the first time on a major issue and made a pretence of causing maximum disruption by organizing stoppages on alternate weeks over a short period. Parents were informed of the dates on which their children should not be sent to school. Non-striking teachers were paid their normal salary for turning up and spending days in empty classrooms catching up on correction or preparation — or in groups in the staffrooms playing bridge or just dozing the hours away.

Candlish refused to take part in the action, adamant in his conviction, as some others were, that a really *effective* strike had to be both selective and prolonged. But he did throw a few pound notes into the box placed in a staffroom to help those who were forgoing their wages.

While all this was happening a committee, under the chairmanship of one Lord Houghton, investigated conditions and salaries. The outcome was the 1974 Houghton Report, which recommended minor improvements in the former and a far from adequate improvement in the latter, but which most teachers, being what they were, accepted, some even with gratitude, apparently oblivious to the fact that spiralling inflation and their customary place at the end of the wage rises queue would soon all but nullify that increase when others quickly received their next one. To achieve any sort of equity they would have required at least double the amount they did get. Apart from their own feeble "unions" and their own lack of drive, another reason for their impotency was their misfortune to be operating in a field which was in no way concerned with making money or being able to offer an immediate solution to pressing problems, because it was a field which didn't present any; after all, education was a long-term process administered by long-winded officials in their long-established talking-shops and crucial mistakes, even if revealed or admitted, which they seldom were, did not unduly worry the public at large; the employment of grossly incompetent teachers did not have parents howling for their dismissal, even when their own children were the victims; different if you had a burst appendix, different too if you were likely to suffer from a shortage of winter fuel or be severely inconvenienced by a transport strike — such goings-on affected the well-being of the nation and soon had the nation clamouring for something to be done, and quickly. But the industrial clout possessed by the medics or the postmen or the firemen was a weapon believed to be sadly lacking in the teachers' armoury. The stops that could be pulled out on the educational organ, if they were pulled out, would emit no more than the tiniest of squeaks. Yet they might have amounted to more than mere squeaks if stoppages of indefinite duration, as proposed by Candlish and his supporters, had been held in certain chosen schools.

During the decades that followed little changed, except for the worse. The Houghton Report of 1974 was followed by the Clegg Report in 1980, and the Clegg Report by the Main Report in 1986, each by its very existence tantamount to an admission that its predecessor, where there was one, had conspicuously failed to put matters right. And then the miraculous happened when, for the first time since the Second World War, Scotland found itself with a surplus of teaching staff.

The miraculous happened not because teaching had become a much more attractive career — rather the reverse was the case — but because a recession had prevented graduates from obtaining posts in professions they would have much preferred. Teaching was still much more remunerative and, some no doubt thought, more uplifting than standing behind a counter selling newspapers or washing dishes in a restaurant. So with the appearance of so many qualified beginners here was the opportunity for improvement, for their lords and masters to fill the gaps they had for so long professed to deplore and to fulfill their earlier promises to reduce class sizes as soon as possible (the theory upheld by some of them, that the number of pupils in a teaching group is of no consequence, that the quality of the instruction alone matters, simply proves that either they had had no classroom experience themselves or were looking for a convenient excuse to leave matters as they were). So the promises, made in the days when schools had started to struggle along with staffs that sometimes reached skeleton proportions, proved to be as empty as the heads of a high proportion of school-leavers. The teachers, continually told in sympathetic terms that there was very little that could be done to lessen their workloads, thought they now had at least some reason to rejoice. They should have known better. The excuse this time was lack of funds and, to drive the point home, they were informed that sackings were imminent.

    Here too was the opportunity to heed the repeated warnings from those responsible for appointing youngsters to business and industry: that educational standards were fast approaching the abysmal, especially with regard to English, whether in written or spoken form: the former pregnant with all the abominations of spelling and grammar imaginable, the latter laced with "yobspeak" utterances — "we ain't", "she come", "they played brilliant", and delivered in such a sloppy manner as to render most of it unfathomable to the normal ear. School-leavers' ability to cope with simple mental arithmetic also came in for much criticism, as did their general knowledge of subjects considered worthy of inclusion in that category. That did not apply to pop groups, football stars or Australian TV soaps.

    As conditions deteriorated — continual changes in curricula, the introduction of various tests sometimes abandoned just when teachers had completed all the spadework, endless and pointless paperwork which further diverted them from the job they were supposed to be doing, mounting indiscipline — it was inevitable that more and more of those engaged in the classroom should give the impression of having thrown in the towel into which they had so miserably snivelled for so long.

Later on, and years into his retirement, Candlish's beliefs continued to be confirmed when members of the NASUWT in England and Wales — contrary to the wishes of the other unions, which were made of similar stuff to their Scottish equivalents — voted to strike in protest against oversized classes. Gillian Shephard, the Education Secretary (one of those who maintained that the number of pupils in a teaching group was unimportant) unashamedly spouted forth the perennial twaddle of 40 years standing: "If teachers absent themselves from the schools they will do their professional status irreparable harm". Another politician, no less a personage than her boss, John Major, joined in to support her with a profound: "Teachers should be in their classrooms imparting knowledge to their pupils, not outside them teaching them bad habits". If these two ever lose their jobs, which at the moment of writing seems likely, they could always apply for full-time positions with the NUT (National Union of Teachers) or, if they prefer Scottish air, with the EIS or the SSTA.

When parents were asked on TV's *Newsnight* what they thought of teachers taking strike action in an effort to get class sizes reduced, they stated their willingness to accept a temporary disruption to their children's education if they were later rewarded with a long-term improvement in classroom instruction.

All this inspired a flow of letters to the Scottish and English press and their general tone suggested that the public was overwhelmingly on the teachers' side. It was pointed out that classes of 30 pupils in 1995 were much harder to handle than the same number a couple of decades before. The withdrawal of corporal punishment had seen to that, but the government had taken no effective steps to address the problem of growing indiscipline. Each year more and more teachers were physically assaulted, more and more of them were forced to take days off in order to partially recover from the debilitating form of stress which was the direct result of their constant fight to try and make themselves heard in classrooms — even primary classrooms — and the demoralizing effect that such a situation can have is known only to those who have to endure it. But more about this later.

Chapter 6
TRAVEL BROADENS THE MIND

While still an assistant at Abergarvie Academy, Candlish had taken two parties of pupils to the Continent (much to Naithsmith's gratification since it was the Principal Teacher of Modern Languages who was normally expected to shoulder this responsibility). On both occasions they went to Germany, first of all to Hamburg, which Candlish had last seen in 1946 when it had still been nothing else but square mile after square mile of ghastly ruins. But now the great Hanseatie port had been completely rebuilt, a gleaming metropolis which revealed hardly a sign of the inferno that had consumed much of it less than a decade before.

Before setting out he had given the members of the party — almost exclusively students of German and all from Years V and VI, a brief illustrated history of Germany's second city. He mentioned its ordeal at the hands of Bomber Command — which was part of its history — and while doing so was rudely interrupted by one Billy McPhail, a rather bumptious adolescent who had suddenly become aware of the world around him and despite his youth already had sure and fixed ideas on everything.

"Why did Hamburg have to be destroyed like that and all those innocent civilians killed? Do you not have that on your conscience, sir?"

Candlish suspected that McPhail had been put up to asking the question by McPhail senior, a clerk in the Education Offices who for some reason thought his position was far more exalted than it was and had already interfered with Candlish in a matter which was none of his concern and had been rebuked accordingly.

"I'll overlook your remark for the time being, McPhail, and perhaps some day after the Higher is over I'll put you straight on a subject about which you obviously know nothing, and are merely echoing what you have heard from a misinformed source."

The second German visit had been to a Rhineland village a few miles south of Bonn and in addition to excursions to the Federal capital itself, where they saw the interiors of both the Bundestag and the Beethovenhaus, other historic towns such as Cologne, Koblenz and Wiesbaden were included in the itinerary.

Those were still days in which few school pupils had ever been abroad and when both they and their parents were appreciative of the opportunity offered. Those who took part were all of above average intelligence and caused Candlish and his helpers only minor problems apart from the occasional accident, if any at all. Most of them made a genuine attempt to speak the language and took an interest in what they saw, so that the staff in charge felt it had all been worthwhile, and had even enjoyed it themselves.

But times had changed; and the new attitudes and modes nurtured by the new society altered the nature of school outings as they altered everything else. Candlish undertook three trips from Glentilloch, all to France or Belgium, and, to demonstrate that such sojourns had ceased to be the prerogative of the academically superior or financially better-off, the authority recommended — or rather insisted — that from an altruistic point of view, by which it really meant a politically correct point of view, non-certificate pupils should make up at least half the total number; and that it would grant substantial monetary assistance to those parents eligible to apply for it.

But we've all seen things that look good in theory, especially political theory, and from the authority's claimed philanthropic standpoint this revised conception of the composition of school parties going abroad could hardly be faulted provided you were not one of the teachers involved, or one of the foreign citizens to be graced by their presence amongst them; Candlish pointed out that he doubted very much whether the type of pupil in question would derive any benefit at all from participating — their indifferent reactions to short visits to places of interest in the local area had proved this time and time again. What he did not doubt was their effect on the welfare of the whole party and the problems they would present to the staff; conducting "certificate pupils" to foreign lands could create difficulties enough, but being saddled with the you-know-whos for a whole week or more he could only look upon with the direst foreboding; in a word — and he made no bones about it — he personally was less concerned with altruistic considerations than he was with hard practicalities, and there was an odds-on chance that some of those who would be allowed to take part were recalcitrants who had already been in trouble both at school and with the Police. (Candlish witnessed what he regarded as the extreme application of this doctrine when, later on in the early nineties, "rehabilitative" safari-type holidays in Kenya were awarded, at the taxpayers' expense, to convicted "joy-riders" and other miscreants: this he saw as the inevitable outcome of the fashionable tendency, sprung from the concept of Comprehensive Education, to sow more and more seed, defective in the first place, on ground mistakenly judged to possess the constituents which would propagate and then foster it. Unhappily weeds continue to breed weeds, even when they share a bed with roses).

His overtures failed to convince; or perhaps they didn't fail, but ideals were at stake; and the reply was as fatuous as it was dismissive:

"Oh, you'll manage, Mr Candlish!"

"I might manage better if I could rope in (he considered the verb appropriate) a few more adults to help with supervision. What about some of you?"

Oh no, that was quite impossible. They had already booked their holidays or were having visitors or had to stay at home to tend their vegetables.

*   *   *

The Rector's advice to Candlish, not that such advice was necessary, was to choose locations not too far distant from the French or Belgian ferry ports to cut down on the amount of time they would have to spend in trains and coaches. Each of the excursions from Glentilloch, so meritoriously egalitarian in their make-up, became progressively more of an ordeal, with the escorting members of staff continually on the qui-vive and rarely able to relax. To make matters worse, even those pupils who occupied a higher than average rung on the IQ ladder seemed to be less interested in what they saw in the foreign country than their predecessors in Germany some years before, while the first desire of the non-academic 15-year olds, at least of the males amongst them, was to be left to their own devices as much as possible and to sneak off into cafés to sample the various brands of wine, although they had received stern warnings, in a deliberately exaggerated fashion, of the tough treatment meted out by French or Belgian police to those guilty of undesirable behaviour in public and of what they could expect once they got back to Glentilloch. They were largely unimpressed by the medieval splendours of Bruges or the arresting beauties of Paris (where they spent a whole day while based at Beauvais) and were attracted more by the dimly-lit bistros just off the main square in the former and the chic mademoiselles parading the broad boulevards of the latter. Nothing unnatural about the latter tendency in maturing teenagers, one might say, but it was something they could do equally well at home, where they did it all the time. One hoped that for once they might just rivet their attention on something else, but with them it was forever first things first, no matter where they were.

When Candlish overhead one of his charges sum up Bruges with an impatient: "Whut a bloody dump! It's a' auld hooses an' bloody canals whaur streets should be," and another, after gazing askance at some passers-by engaged in animated conversation, spout forth the unanswerable query: "Whut fur they cannae speak Inglish like we dae, sur?" he found himself calculating the number of days that had still to be endured.

On one occasion, while they were staying in Beauvais, one of the shining lights of IIIC — yes, imagine them in a hotel — came charging in through the main door as he did through every door in Glentilloch High School, and proceeded to collide head-on with the proprietor's pride and joy, a large bust of Napoleon I, which stood on a pedestal in the foyer — or at least had done up till then. Of all the blows which had befallen Bonaparte in his long and tempestuous career, surely none had been as shattering as this; and as he bit the dust — or rather the linoleum — the ominous crash brought the proprietor and others, including Candlish, running from all points of the compass to find out if a wall had collapsed. But they were not held in suspense for long: at first the erstwhile Emperor of the French was nowhere to be seen, certainly not in his usual place and in his original form, for he lay all over the floor in bits and pieces, the emphasis being on bits, and of the pieces the largest was the imperial nose. But his protagonist had not escaped the skirmish unscathed and was slowly and painfully hauling himself to his feet and looking even more dumbstruck than he did normally.

Monsieur Leduc, an unashamed xenophobe who at every opportunity singled out the UK in particular as the target for his pet hate (although this did not permit his other obsession — money — to preclude the acceptance of British guests) was convinced that this was an act of outrageous sabotage against him and his hero, not to mention *la Belle France*, and probably instigated by Candlish himself who, in spite of his profuse apologies, angered him further by remarking that the bust had hardly been an *objet d'art* in the first place and that he would no doubt obtain a replacement from some junk shop. Monsieur Leduc vehemently disagreed and quoted a ridiculous figure as compensation; but Candlish reminded him that the item had been fashioned from cheap plaster and handed him £15 in francs as an immediate and final settlement (fortunately he had taken out insurance to meet with the high likelihood of such an eventuality). Yet Monsieur Leduc's prized possession might well have been of real value, and when Candlish chastised the culprit, telling him that he had reduced to nondescript rubble an effigy of the great Napoleon, he looked genuinely surprised:

"Eh? It didnae even look like Napoleon, sur."

The only Napoleon he knew was the one in the TV series "The Man from Uncle".

*   *   *

The ferry crossings were perhaps the biggest ordeal of all, especially if the sea was rough and the boat crowded; trying to keep such an unruly pack confined to a small section of the deck, preferably close to a toilet, was anything but easy, and almost justified tethering them all together; hence the sighs of relief from their chaperons each time the French (and in particular the British) port came into view. Yet the company of such a bunch of scallywags did occasionally provide some welcome hilarity: once when half-way across on the outward journey, Candlish noticed that one Joe Todd, who had a marked propensity for putting his foot, or rather his tongue, right into it, whether it was on a pitching Channel steamer or on his rounds of Glentilloch, was looking rather sorry for himself and clasping his ear. Thinking he had perhaps had a slight argument with an uncompromising bulwark or whatever (there was a fair wind blowing) Candlish called him over and asked what was the trouble:

"Oh, that big sambo across there cracked me yin across the lug."

"Why? What had you done?"

"Nothin', sur. He's sellin' tubes o' somethin' he says stops ye gettin' a' burnt wi' the sun."

"So?"

"A said the stuff didnae seem tae hae helped him much, an' he clattered me."

* * *

Thanks to even more generous grants awarded by the authority a phenomenal number of pupils — 88 — enrolled for Candlish's third expedition from Glentilloch; and since a large proportion of those involved threatened to equal or excel their predecessors' penchant for fragmenting items such as busts of historic personages or of provoking retaliatory action of the kind effected by the coloured gentleman peddling anti-sunburn lotion, Candlish refused point-blank to shepherd them en masse; in any case it would have been practically impossible to find an hotel both able and willing to put up, and to put up with, a sizeable slice of adolescent humanity as unpredictable as it was unprepossessing. So he did the only feasible thing and split them into two groups, with three members of staff in charge of each. He also knew only too well that the incidence of misbehaviour could usually be measured in direct proportion to the total number of bodies.

The first batch travelled by private coach to Dover and hence to Boulogne to spend their week in a small coastal resort nearby (obviously not one which aspired to the standards of Paris-Plage) and on its way back was passed in mid-Channel by the second contingent bound for the same hotel. Having just disgorged the latter at Dover the coach sat there awaiting the arrival of their homeward-bound schoolmates to transport them back to Glentilloch, whence it would depart again for Dover about six days later to bring the others home. The operation took on all the characteristics of a military exercise and the hotel those of a transit camp; scarcely had its elderly owners time to gulp down a recuperative calvados after the evacuation of their premises by the first squad when they were besieged by the second, led by Candlish himself, who found Monsieur and Madame supporting each other on the front steps. Their valiant attempt to produce a welcoming smile did not, unfortunately, progress beyond a painful contortion of the facial muscles. And who could censure them? When you had just repelled one raucous invasion the very last thing you wanted on this earth was another following immediately in its wake. Perhaps it all reminded them of what they had gone through in not too distant Caen a quarter of a century before; but, as on that occasion, they gritted their teeth, for after all it was to their advantage in the end: more luscious lolly beneath their Gallic floorboards.

Yet, if you disregarded frayed nerves and ringing ears, the total damage on this visit amounted to little more than a few broken pieces of china in the dining room, a bedroom carpet smothered in the feathers which should by rights have remained the contents of pillow slips, and a curtain yanked from its runner by a 15-year old who liked to emulate his hero, Tarzan (once again Candlish had to pay for the damage and claim for reimbursement). The most serious infraction of the *Code Napoléon* was committed on the penultimate day by the removal of a couple of life-belts from their housings on the seafront and their erratic propulsion by whacking sweeps of the hand along the length of the promenade, just as their grandfathers had done with their "girds" (normally discarded bicycle wheels) when they were 7 or 8-year olds; an assault which spurred alert and agile burghers out for their morning stroll into spontaneous evasive action, and caused those neither alert nor agile to cry out as they suffered shock to ageing legs and thighs as they involuntarily diverted the speeding missiles elsewhere. Those untouched or unshaken hastened to summon the nearest gendarme, who decided that the transgressors, who merely gawped when he questioned them in his native tongue and made unintelligible sounds in reply, must be inmates on a day out from one of those institutions which look after juveniles with a tendency to indulge in bizarre behaviour. As he gazed frantically around in search of some attendant in a white coat, mere chance had dictated that at that very moment Candlish and one of his assistants were killing two birds, as it were, by enjoying a whiff of sea air and simultaneously carrying out a bit of supervision. On noting that an upholder of the law had grabbed two of their charges by the scruff of the neck they hurried over to investigate. Candlish had to make the most of the Auld Alliance, of the play habits of Scottish children, even older ones (not mentioning that the "gird" had been defunct for years), and of his own diplomatic expertise, to stop things going any further. They were all returning home the next day, he said, and as far as he was concerned they would not be coming back. Good news for the town's gendarmerie, good news for its citizenry. Good news for everyone.

* * *

By the mid-seventies the vast majority of pupils, including those of whom you might have expected more, regarded school parties to a cultural or semi-cultural neighbourhood as a poor second to Benidorm or Majorca, venues which they preferred even if the presence of their parents imposed unwelcome restrictions on their freedom of action. The Bonns and the Bruges were regarded as barely tolerable alternatives; and it came to the point that it was no longer wise to give them an hour or two on their own because this, Candlish had discovered, could lead to objectionable behaviour, which in some cases included heavy consumption of alcohol; not surprising, therefore, that some hotels were refusing to accommodate youngsters from British, and especially English, schools — the latter probably aping the "lager lout" cult — on account of their disruptive effect on other guests and their lack of respect for others' property; and if nothing more serious happened than it did — and some of the things that had happened were serious enough — during the trips conducted by Candlish from Glentilloch, this was due entirely to the tireless and tiring vigilance exercised throughout by him and his assistants and not to any feeling of gratitude or sense of responsibility on the part of those being conducted. If the teachers in command had been of the fast-growing trendy breed he might have had dealings with more than a mere insurance company.

The deepest reservoir, whether its contents be water or forbearance, can be ultimately drained, and Candlish decided that enough was enough, that his days as an unpaid educational tour guide were over. From now on he and Eileen would go to the Continent alone, or perhaps with their own children, but emphatically not with any who belonged to someone else.

Chapter 7
CHANCE ENCOUNTERS

During the summer holidays of 1967 Candlish attended a week-long course in Aberdeen on new trends in the teaching of Modern Languages. This gave him opportunity for both formal and informal discussion with the man in charge, HM Chief Inspector of these subjects.

A few weeks later he received an unexpected invitation from the Scottish Certificate of Education Examination Board (later to be shortened to the Scottish Examination Board) to set the Ordinary Grade paper in French for 1969. This he accepted without hesitation, aware that such an undertaking would enable him to acquire an in-depth appreciation of the French "O" Grade and that this knowledge would be invaluable to himself, his teaching staff and their pupils. (The Board — and the opinion was universal amongst teachers — displayed for some inexplicable reason, an almost obsessive reluctance to reveal anything about its inner workings). He was then asked to mark 50 papers for the 1968 Examination and to attend the Markers' Meeting to see for himself the rôle he would play as setter in front of some 100 markers the following year.

It should perhaps be pointed out at this stage that with the increasing numbers of presentations in all subjects at both "O" and "H" Grades, the Inspectorate had become no longer capable of handling the external examinations; accordingly, apart from a core of permanent and part-time staff at the Board's Causewayside Headquarters — it was to move to new and much larger premises in Dalkeith in 1975 — all of the work concerned with setting, correction and subsequent procedures vis-à-vis the written papers became the responsibility of serving (and some retired) teachers, with a sprinkling of college and university lecturers.   Oral tests, where applicable, were conducted mainly by the latter.

Setting any examination paper was and probably always will be, an exacting business, and no more exacting than in a modern language. Its composition called for the complete absence of any ambiguity either in the questions themselves or in the answers expected, or as near to its complete absence as could possibly be foreseen, otherwise the marking would suffer as regards both accuracy and consistency. But in addition other criteria had to be strictly observed. The length of the language passages, whether for translation into English or interpretation or whatever, had to fall within narrowly prescribed limits; the style of the language and its degree of difficulty (syntax, idiom, vocabulary) had all to conform to the standard apposite at the time; the suitability of the subject matter was also important: candidates must not be upset by topics such as death or violence or by the inclusion of any material which might prove disturbing to certain individuals amongst them. All these prerequisites served to limit the setting field considerably, and in an era when the mass media were devoting more and more coverage to destruction and barbarity, Candlish was inclined to the view that the Board was guilty of a certain naïveté in rejecting themes which were relatively mild in comparison and would have been most unlikely to perturb the most sensitive of modern teenagers; he would rather have had a ban put on subject matter which was definitely to the advantage of one or other of the sexes, but this precaution appeared to apply only in extreme cases.

Such manifold requirements and limitations made the task a long and difficult one and the final product had to be chiselled, and then honed until Candlish could claim it to be as fault-free as it could *foreseeably* be; foreseeably, because an exam on a literary subject cannot be devised on precise scientific lines. It cannot be rendered coldly clinical and if it turns out to be essentially reliable it is virtually a work of art, for, like all works of art, it is never without blemishes, however slight; the most minor of flaws invited further difficulties in the marking which, as we shall learn, was hazardous enough without them.

His next task was the provision of detailed Marking Instructions. Due to the tremendous breadth of expression offered by the mother tongue, these had to be particularly exhaustive for the translation passage since a French phrase could often be turned acceptably into English in a host of different ways, and all those he could think of were entered in the Acceptable column of the Instructions. Another column headed Partly Acceptable listed such items and stated the required deduction, usually one half mark, while a third tabulated what would no doubt be common but wholly unacceptable versions.

When the "O" Grade Paper itself and the corresponding Marketing Instructions had been completed to Candlish's satisfaction he sent everything, as instructed, to the person (a Principal Teacher like himself) setting the "H" Grade, who perused it for any shortcomings and then returned it with his comments, and Candlish did likewise with his. The only infallible way — if infallible it could ever be — of checking the Marketing Instructions was to write out the answers to the questions before looking at those expected by the setter and then to compare the two and make a note of any disparities. With these adjusted both Paper and Marking Instructions were sent to the Chief Examiner who added his own comments or suggested any changes he thought desirable (during consultation with the setter). He then sent copies to each member of a Modern Languages Panel who pronounced their verdict. By this stage the Paper was rarely rejected in whole, sometimes in part, but more often than not it was accepted as it stood, or with only one or two minor alterations. Once finalised it went off to the printer.

As soon as the candidates had sat their examination it was the duty of the invigilator in charge of the paper — normally a retired professional man or woman — to return all the scripts to the Board without delay. These were quickly re-addressed and sent out, together with a copy of the Marking Instructions, to the appropriate markers, each receiving a batch of 200-300. They were asked to mark as many as possible, provisionally and in pencil, before attending the Markers' Meeting about a week later, sometimes held at Board Headquarters in Dalkeith, but usually in Edinburgh, where all sorts of accommodation had to be utilized all over the city, including church halls and even their freezing basements. The markers were also instructed to note on the Instructions any difficulties they had encountered or points with which they disagreed.

The more work the setter had put into his Marking Instructions the more smoothly the meeting progressed and the more consistent the subsequent correction proved to be. Each question was dealt with in turn, and any objections from markers to the expected answers, whether stated to be acceptable or unacceptable, were considered and amendments made to the Instructions if necessary. The English language being as expansive as it is and as grammatically controversial as it has become, there were always possible renderings which had not occurred to the setter and these were placed in the appropriate column; some of the penalties were increased or decreased; any anomalies were eliminated and on points where markers were at variance a decision was reached by a simple show of hands. At the close of the meeting all were reminded that they had to adhere strictly to every decision taken, even if they strongly disagreed with it.

Marking a huge pile of examination papers is a wearing and lengthy business which can strain nerves almost to breaking point. In view of the intense concentration required it must rank as one of the few boring activities in the execution of which you cannot allow your thoughts to stray elsewhere. It has also been known to make people physically sick.

The fee paid for marking a script was based on the time the

examinees were allowed to complete it, and although the Board was continually expressing its thanks to markers for the invaluable and responsible work they were doing, its gratitude was hardly reflected in the scale of remuneration which was so uninvitingly low that volunteers were often difficult to find (vacancies were advertised in the national press) and many tended to be young and inexperienced teachers desperate to make some extra cash. Some of those of more advanced years took it on once or twice — usually once — to gain a useful insight into the workings of the examination or to accrue some holiday money for that summer. But once was generally enough; for where the cash bonanza was the main driving force they found it fell far short of being a just reward for the effort they had expended and hardly had them longing for a repeat of the agony the following year. Other considerations apart they told themselves they would have earned much more going from door to door selling dusters and toilet brushes. One competent but disgusted first-time marker of Candlish's acquaintance phoned him one night, after receiving his fee, to say that according to his calculations he had been paid half the hourly rate of the elderly man who looked after his neighbour's garden. He swore he would never grace a Markers' Meeting with his presence again. Candlish said he didn't blame him.

    He didn't blame him because although on the whole Candlish had come to admire the Board for its meticulously orchestrated programme and for a policy aimed at, if not altogether achieving, complete fairness in all departments — as we shall discover presently — his chief criticism focused on its arbitrary method of appointing its markers. There seemed to him to be little point in demanding near perfection in the examination paper itself and then letting loose on it an appreciable number of individuals — even one was one too many — whose poor quality of marking provided the contaminated seed which became the root of all subsequent problems; in a word all the setter's sweated efforts could so easily be vitiated by laxity on the party of those entrusted with the correction. It could be said with much justification that as a direct consequence of its parsimonious rates of payment the Board got the markers it deserved, and that it was fortunate in not getting more of the same inferior calibre. Perish the thought.

Despite the fact that the Board stipulated that candidates' scripts should not leave the security of the marker's home, and never taken into public places, this ruling was openly flouted. Papers were "marked" in busy, jolting trains and buses; they were "marked" in school staffrooms and even in classrooms with possible bedlam reigning if an undisciplined group of pupils was present; they were "marked" after an evening spent at the local pub, or with the TV switched on, or when the marker was dead tired or simply in the wrong frame of mind for the absolute concentration required. It was even suspected once, and with very good reason, that several of a marker's papers had been corrected by his spouse, also a French teacher. The permutations were practically endless.

Markers guilty of any of the aforementioned infractions of the SCE code took the view that they considered themselves quite justified in sacrificing no more of their free time as appeared commensurate with the miserable emoluments with which they were rewarded. Unethical and inexcusable? Yes, of course. But to some extent *understandable* in the circumstances?

It should be emphasised, however, that the majority of markers insisted on a quiet and private setting for their work, concentrated 100% on what they were doing and worried about their accuracy, especially in the essay question. Yet the unpalatable fact remains that slapdash correction on the part of a significant minority — whose primary concern was to get the damned things finished and out of the way — should never have been tolerated. Why it needn't have been tolerated we shall endeavour to show in due course.

All corrected papers had to be returned to the Board by a specified date, generally three weeks later. As they started to arrive in fleets of Post Office vans an army of part-time sorters, mostly female, were kept busy recording the raw marks allotted to each candidate by the marker and filing away the thousands and thousands of scripts from hundreds of educational institutions all over Scotland. These had to be instantly available for the procedures which would follow. Although this was easily the busiest time of all at the Board Offices hardly a day of the year passed without a multitude of forms going out to, or coming in from, schools and colleges, invigilators, setters and markers. The whole process amounted to an extraordinary feat of organization and timing and it was a rare occurrence indeed if anything went wrong — or missing. The Post Office too deserved some recognition for its efficiency.

The raw marks referred to above were regarded as a sort of *point de départ* and in many cases would be altered at least once, and possibly twice, by the team of examiners

(again usually serving teachers) who would carry out various procedures and eventually produce the final mark and thus the Grading A, B, C, D or E for each examinee. D or E meant failure.

The first of these procedures was called Standardization and it was here that bad marking was conspicuous by its too frequent presence. Each member of the team selected at random a small number of scripts, usually five, from each marker's assignment and re-marked them with a green pen (it is much easier to mark an untouched script than one already covered in red ink) and after a week thus engaged Candlish and his colleagues complained of mental fatigue and eyes that were definitely feeling the effects of constant strain. The discrepancy between the marker's mark and the examiner's mark was recorded and where it was deemed to be quite tolerable (-1, 0, -2, -1, 0) an average was taken (in the example quoted -1) which was termed the Standardization Factor and applied by the administrative staff to all the other papers corrected by the same marker   That appeared to be straightforward enough, but what remedial action could be taken when the result was +6, -5, +4, 0, -7? or even, now and again, a monstrosity such as -12, +10, 0, -15, +6? Obviously none by way of a Standardization Factor, and the scripts had to be remarked in their entirety by someone else willing to take it on (and the work paid for for a second time). Normally the maverick marker was informed of his remissness and told that he would not be invited to participate in future. All this, of course, entailed extra work and delay.   But then if you start off with dodgy parts to your engine you can expect trouble along the way. And the most delaying — and largely preventable — breakdown of the lot was marking which varied between that which was less than satisfactory to that which was downright appalling.

    Once the appropriate alterations — and there were plenty of them — had been made to the raw mark the next important procedure was Borderline Scrutiny.   But before this operation could begin the Principal Examiner in each subject, the setter and sometimes the Director of the Board himself had first to get together and decide on the passmark (not an immutable 50% which those not in the know supposed it to be, but modifiable and generally a few marks less). It was in fact determined by one or two different factors and not least, in those subjects with large numbers of candidates, by the reasonable assumption that the spread of intellect was basically similar from one year to the next and hence roughly the same number of passes should be awarded — in the neighbourhood of 70%. So a quick calculation provided the passmark which, one might say, was worked out backwards; and everything considered this was a quick and accurate way of finding it.

    Obviously this method was unworkable in subjects where the number of presentations was much smaller and which necessitated a different approach.   In what might be termed extreme cases —

Italian, Russian, Navigation — it was more often than not the setter who had marked all of the few papers himself and who had the final say in deciding whether a candidate be granted a pass or not.

Borderline Scrutiny in the principal subjects presented a further painstaking task for the team of examiners. The scripts of all candidates who had failed by one or two marks were extracted from their bundles and perused on the chance of finding the mark or marks required to award a C pass. As far as a modern language was concerned this was most likely to be achieved by a re-reading of the essay, since this question was assessed in bands of five marks from 0 to 50; so if the examiner judged that an essay should have been placed one category higher, then the examinee was credited with a further five marks, which meant he was through with something to spare. If the examiner couldn't make up his mind whether an essay ought to be upped a grade or not he asked the person working next to him to read it, and if he said it didn't merit any increase or that he wasn't sure either, then a search had to be made elsewhere in the paper for that crucial single or double mark.

But this gambit, advantageous as it undoubtedly was to some, acted as a double-edged sword by denying any similar favours to those who fell short of the passmark by three, four or five marks; no Borderline Scrutiny for them, and it must have occurred that they included several candidates who had also written an essay which qualified for an additional five marks and therefore a pass. And of course there existed a further possibility: someone who had just scraped through by a mark or two might well have produced an essay which ought to have been placed in a lower band, in which case he would have failed. But passed scripts were never scrutinized, only those falling just below the passmark. And so it follows that some passed who should have failed and, even worse, others failed who should have passed.

In no exam can you ever exclude the capricious dispositions

of Lady Luck, who smiles benignly on some and does not take so kindly to others; nor can you totally exclude fluctuations in marking, even by those who display the greatest degree of vigilance. (This was a sober fact of which Candlish was graphically reminded towards the end of his first Borderline Scrutiny when a member of his team told him he had just been thoroughly shaken on re-reading a failed candidate's essay in the hope of finding the couple of marks which would mean a pass. The marker had awarded 15, which, he thought, was severe and accordingly he had upped it to 20. He was then quite horrified on suddenly noticing that it was he himself who was the original marker. Different day? Different mood? Different way of seeing things?) Yet decisions had to be taken and you couldn't go on having judges judging the judges for ever. But travesties of the nature of those recounted in the preceding paragraphs belonged to another category and could be avoided by changes in the mechanism proposed by Candlish and his associates and will be outlined at the end of this chapter.

Borderline Scrutiny was not the end of the Board's efforts to assist the unsuccessful candidate. He who learned some weeks later, when the results had been posted out, that only one of the fail grades (D or E) in a certain subject was his miserable lot, all hope was not yet lost because schools were allowed to appeal on his behalf if they could supply written evidence (internal examinations, for instance) which strongly suggested that the pupil really ought to have passed. Although this evidence was sometimes inspected it was seldom regarded as being reliable — often rightly so — and the telling factor was his position on the Order of Merit form previously sent in by his school; if he occupied a higher place on it than others of his teaching group who had comfortably passed, then the award was normally granted.

Provision was also made for those who had been subjected to "Adverse Circumstances" just before or during the examination. If a near relative had suddenly died or the school had provided proof of some painful medical disorder afflicting the candidate or if low-flying jets had repeatedly disturbed the peace of the examination room, these could be looked upon as disruptive influences and taken into account. Unfortunately many of the claims received were of a minor nature or completely absurd and served only to waste the Board's time; some were quite amusing and at least afforded a few seconds of welcome relief to those engaged in a type of labour not exactly renowned for its moments of levity.

Experienced examiners — and Candlish could claim to be one of these — obviously accrued an intimate knowledge of the Board's *modus operandi* and were in a position to offer recommendations which would make it, in their opinion, more just and efficient. They did not dispute the fact that the Board went to much trouble in performing an exceedingly difficult and delicate task and if they were unappreciative of this, which they certainly were not, they were clearly reminded of it when they chatted with "professional markers" from South of the Border — retired teachers who spent much of their time correcting papers for the various Boards in England and the one in Scotland. These people never ceased to express their unstinted admiration for the lengths to which the SCE was prepared to go in conducting its examinations. Candlish and his co-examiners thought they must be exaggerating somewhat (this was around 1970) when they said that down South you simply applied to be a marker and when the exam had taken place a bundle of scripts arrived one day on your doorstep and you got down to it with your red pen. Yes, just like that; no Marking Instructions as we knew them in Scotland, no Markers' Meetings, no devices for processing raw marks, no Appeals or Adverse Circumstances or anything else. You simply marked the papers and sent them back. Small wonder that such a system, if that is not too flattering a term for it, gave rise to cases like that of the girl who failed her "O" Level abysmally with one Board, went soon afterwards to live in an area under the auspices of another, re-sat and came out with flying colours in the form of an A. By all accounts the slothful approach in England was quite incomprehensible and more than a little frightening.

But it is rather naïve to smugly congratulate yourself on your own methods just because they compare favourably with the worst; and although Candlish and his colleagues had much to say in praise of the Scottish Board's carefully thought-out practices and were only too cognizant of the difficulties inherent in conducting a national examination, with fairness to all and smooth running the main objectives, they were at the same time well aware of one or two procedural defects; in their opinion, and it was an opinion derived from long and penetrating observation, the most glaring of these defects occurred, as we have perceived, in Standardization, and all of it arising from the employment of incompetent markers; and in Borderline Scrutiny where, as we have also noted, the method used, for all its good intentions, could hardly be described as ideal. As matters stood the candidates received their results and accepted them without question, ignorant of the fact that their D fail ought to have been a C pass — or their C pass a D fail. Something, they felt, ought to be done about it.

Accordingly Candlish and some who were as concerned as he was about the need for a rethink in these departments, submitted to the Chief Examiner in Modern Languages their well reasoned argument for the abolition of both Standardization and Borderline Scrutiny on the grounds that such procedures might appear superficially desirable but in reality were deceptively fallacious. They pointed out that the Standardization Factor, far from being a wonderful panacea which adjusted the raw marks to a high level of credibility, depended entirely on the five scripts which had been selected from the marker's pile. If five others had been chosen a different Factor might well have — in all probability would have — been applied to all his scripts. Everything depended on how, where, when and by whom the papers had been marked. This was a national examination and should have none of the trappings of a national lottery.

Secondly, despite the commendable motives behind Borderline Scrutiny, this was an operation in which Lady Fortune was again allowed to play too big a part and for that reason entailed gross miscarriages of justice.

Both procedures, it was maintained, were, at best, ingenuous forms of window-dressing in which the packaging outdid the content; and, at worst, whirligigs of chance, advantageous to some and the reverse to others. Their virtues were more apparent than real, and they should be abandoned forthwith.

In their stead they proposed that all correction be undertaken by hand-picked Principal Teachers and others who were known for their conscientiousness and their expertise; they should be selected and invited to take on the job and offered remuneration which would reflect the importance of the work; and by that they meant more than the doubling or the trebling of the current rates. Even then it would cost little more, if any more at all, thanks to the removal of teams of examiners whose services would be no longer required, but in any event why spoil everything for a hap'orth or two? A Markers' Meeting would still be necessary, but that would be enough in itself; no need now, thanks to the accuracy and the consistency of the correction, for the laborious and the unjust and the expensive machinery of Standardization and Borderline Scrutiny. Simplification and rectification would go hand in hand. With any examination being what it was, injustices would not be totally eradicated, but they would be reduced to as low a level as anyone could realistically expect.

Regular enquiries as to the reactions to their proposals gave them scant cause for hope: "They're being considered". Apparently they were still being considered several years later, by which time the "O" Grade had been replaced by a new and radical "Standard" Grade and the "Higher " Grade revised, but with the same marking procedures retained. But by then Candlish was no longer engaged by the Board in his previous capacity and, as we shall see, had moved on, examination-wise, into other spheres.

Chapter 8
EGOS

Having finally managed to buy a house in Abergarvie the Candlishs had continued to live there after Iain had become Principal Teacher at Glentilloch; after all, the distance was not great, and staying put meant no disruption to his two children's education; furthermore both Candlish and Eileen were happy where they were and had no desire to move with all the bother that entailed. And travelling had its compensations: Candlish appreciated being back home in Abergarvie each evening; he was far removed from all the pupils he had already seen during the course of the day and of whom he preferred to see no more until the next; continuing to reside there gave him a welcome feeling of anonymity, which spared him all the "Hello sir!" greetings and the stares — and sometimes worse from the yobs — which are the unenviable lot of the teacher based in a smallish country town as soon as he ventures over his doorstep.

Their son Rory, now in his fourth year at Abergarvie Academy, had his heart set on becoming a pilot with the RAF, an ambition kindled in part by what his father had told him about his own flying career and the experiences he had had, albeit under circumstances which Candlish prayed his son would never know.

Amongst the academic qualifications essential for acceptance was the possession of a good school certificate, which must include Mathematics to at least the "O" Grade (in England the "O" Level) standard. Maths, unfortunately, had never been one of Rory's strong points.

So when Candlish got home one day to find both son and wife somewhat down in the dumps, he immediately asked what was wrong.

"We got our Maths papers back today. Big Bert told me I won't be presented." (Bert Rawlings was the Principal Teacher).

"What? What mark did you get?"

"46%".

Candlish almost chocked. Apparently the régime at Abergarvie was no more benevolent than he had known it some years before: the same old brigade of despots calling the same old odds, unaffected by the falling standards and the lower SCE passmarks which signalled the need for a corresponding change in policy to all but them and their like. Their setting and marking remained as off-beam and as tyrannical as ever.

"Don't worry, son. I'll get on the phone to him."

Which he did — right away.

"Look, Bert, I want Rory to sit his "O" Grade Maths."

"No, he doesn't stand a chance."

"How in heaven's name can you say that? How can you be so bloody sure about things? He gets 46% in January with three months teaching still to come before sitting an exam which will be far easier than yours and less strictly marked and ..."

"Nonsense! I repeat — he hasn't the ghost of a chance. That's all there is to be said."

"Oh no, it isn't. Now look here. I'm not an ignorant and timid member of the public easily hoodwinked by such as you. I know what goes on at the Exam Board and I also know what goes on in certain departments at Abergarvie. And anyway you are as aware as I am, or should be, that you can't stop him sitting. But I just don't understand your attitude in making no allowance for falling standards. The big difference between you and me and others like me is that we give even highly doubtful pupils the chance to sit while you and your kind give them no chance at all. I present every youngster who has scored around 30% in the Prelim. — and that is on SCE standards, not on something away above them. If only one in twenty of them passes then I regard that pass as a bonus, whereas you would look on such a presentation as a disaster with 19 failures.

And Rory isn't even a potential failure with his present 46%. Rather is he an almost certain pass."

"I gave my decision to Rory today and it remains the same. I've always had a 100% pass and I mean it to stay that way."

"For Christ's sake, man, you've never had a 100% pass in your life. You can claim a 100% pass only if you present everyone and no-one fails. So to satisfy your own silly little ego, which should be your last consideration, you are quite prepared to sacrifice a lot of children's careers? Does that not bother you? What kind of a man are you?"

"Don't be offensive. As far as I'm concerned the matter is closed."

"By God, it isn't, not as far as *I'm* concerned."

Candlish knew that no pupil could be refused presentation with a mark of 46% in January. Still seething over Rawlings' intransigence he phoned the Rector, whom of course he knew from his own days at Abergarvie.

He explained the situation politely but determinedly and Rory's name went down on the list.

And he passed with a B.

*   *   *

But that was not the end of the matter. At a school Careers Convention Rory was told that the RAF was receiving more applicants for pilot training than it required and therefore it could afford to raise the entrance qualifications. It looked as if an O Grade Maths might no longer be good enough. He would have a far better chance with a Higher.

The boy gave his father the disquieting news.

"Right, go and tell Rawlings tomorrow that you wish to do Higher next year. With a B in "O" Grade you should be alright."

"He'll kill me! Can't you handle it, dad?"

"If necessary, yes, but first you ask yourself. You've already proved him wrong once and it's just possible he has mended his ways. We'll see."

But the answer was very positively in the negative. Rory tried to explain why it was so important that he upped his "O" Grade to a Higher. But all he got in reply was a "Go away boy, and don't be so silly."

This time, instead of using the phone, Candlish went to see him — which, in view of his prevailing mood, made Eileen slightly apprehensive.

He argued the point that it was generally accepted that a pupil with a B in an "O" Grade subject had every chance of at least a C in Higher. But once again the man was not for turning:

"There's a huge difference between "O" and "H" you know."

"Yes, I do know. I should by now. There is in French as well. And there is also a huge difference between the D awarded Rory by you in the Prelim. and the B awarded him by the Board.

"It's different with Higher. A candidate with a D in "O" Grade would never get a C in Higher."

"For Christ's sake, man, it was *you* who gave the D. The Board gave him a B. It's their standards that matter, not yours. Look, the boy needs his Higher Maths to get into an RAF flying school and to make sure he does I'm even prepared to get him some private tuition. But I'm telling you that, as before, he's going to sit. Good evening to you."

And he stamped out.

The Rector appeared to be less receptive to Candlish's arguments than on the previous occasion and he suspected that Rawlings had accused his boss of usurping his authority with regard to presentations. But when Candlish threatened dire action of one kind or another he acquiesced and his son joined a Higher Maths section due to sit the exam the following year. To try to make a pass as certain as possible Candlish did get him some private lessons.

The January Preliminary again produced a D; but surprisingly — or perhaps not — his name went down on the presentation list.

He passed with a C. On making some judicious enquiries at the Board Offices during one of his spells of duty there, Candlish learned that it had been a safe one, nearer a B than a D.

Eileen's fears about her husband's belligerent attitude towards Rawlings were almost substantiated one evening when they met face to face in the town. Rawlings felt he had to say something:

"I simply don't understand how your son passed. Must have been an administrative error somewhere at the Board. I suppose these things must happen now and again."

It was only due to a supreme effort of will that Candlish kept his hands off him. Instead he told him what a selfish fascist bastard he was and hoped he would end up as all fascists should, and usually did.

His irritation with Rawlings and his unacceptable methods had been further increased by a remark Rory had let slip out just after the results had been published: some of his classmates in Higher Maths had been better than he was but had been refused presentation. Candlish intended writing to higher authority to reveal the educationally criminal activities of at least one school, and possibly of others as well. But Eileen's sudden illness shoved everything else into the background. Something far wrong with her blood.

Her condition fluctuated between periods of almost complete incapacitation, when she had to be hospitalized following the administration of horrendous drugs, and merciful periods of near normality when she could cope quite adequately at home.

Chapter 9
FRENCH FOR THE FRY

In the field of teaching, imposition followed upon imposition with the same certainty as night follows day.

Candlish had been forewarned by the Rector that an early meeting would be held at which the Director, some Primary Heads and Candlish himself would be present. The subject to be discussed — although apparently already a *fait accompli* — was the introduction of French into the Glentilloch primaries and into those in the area which also fed their pupils into the High School. The Scottish Education Department intended this evolutionary venture to serve as a pilot scheme which had solid backing from the Inspectorate. It was assumed that Glentilloch and the other Scottish secondaries chosen would welcome the part they would play in the experiment as a privilege, nay an honour. That type of parlance never augured well for a start.

The Director began by stating that a growing number of educationalists, in consequence of the UK's increasing role in European affairs and our poor reputation on the Continent as linguists, believed that the situation could be markedly improved if children were introduced to a modern language long before they reached secondary school age, probably when about eight years old. They were then good imitators, bursting with eagerness, and less self-conscious. Primary staff with a Higher or even an "O" Grade pass in the language would be well able to cope with the elementary standard envisaged: everything would be oral, nothing written, and of course no formal grammar, nothing to dampen their enthusiasm; it would all be devised as entertainment with pupils participating in little playlets and sketches — acting as sellers of fruit and vegetables or as policemen giving directions to tourists or as purveyors of useful information at airports and railway stations. All tremendous fun for all concerned, and so rewarding. It was estimated that two half-hour sessions per week would have them all chattering away like their opposite numbers across the Channel in no time at all.

One of the Primary Heads said he doubted whether any of his staff would be either willing or capable of taking on a task for which they might feel they were quite unqualified. Which they were.

"I've thought of that, " responded the Director. "This is where Mr Candlish comes in. What the primary teachers will need is a sort of refresher course, conversational, of course, for a week or two before we can implement the scheme. Can you organise this, Mr Candlish? I would also expect you to visit the primaries regularly to offer advice where required and to report back to me on how things are going. All right?"

Eileen had had a bad night and Candlish little sleep:

"No! Quite frankly I cannot say I am happy about my rôle in all this. You are well aware of the situation here with regard to shortage of staff. None of us has hardly a moment to call his own and I am surprised that some of the more fortunate schools were not approached rather than us. I haven't enough time to do my job as it is."

"But this will not interfere with your timetable. The primary teachers will come to you, say twice a week for an hour after 4 o'clock."

"No, but it will interfere with other things. And my timetable will be disrupted if I have to go out during the day visiting primary schools. And a further point: there must be some of the smaller country schools which will not have a single teacher with any French at all, so their pupils are going to feel disadvantaged when they come here. But what is far more worrying is the bad habits which will have developed amongst those who do get French — I am thinking of poor pronunciation in particular, which will be difficult to eradicate. Unteaching something like this is a far harder job than starting from scratch. If you want my honest opinion I feel rather sceptical about the whole thing. It would be more worthwhile giving them lessons in basic English, which they don't seem to get."

"I am sorry to hear that, Mr Candlish, but I am afraid we are committed and will have to get on with it. Have you or anyone else any more questions?"

"Yes," Candlish continued, "I have. I trust that the essential equipment will be forthcoming and that there will be enough of it. Apart from oranges and Brussel sprouts and policemen's helmets they're going to need to hear real French voices on tape, large wall charts for the acquisition of vocabulary and other aids as well."

"That's being taken care of. We're ordering a new Nuffield Course which has just come on the market and of course the schools will each be provided with tape recorders and any other equipment necessary."

"Another point: you said that the children will have two half-hour sessions per week. It would be far more preferable to have a 10-minute session every day to ensure continuity and to keep their interest from flagging. Regular practice and frequent repetition of the same material is all-important. That's how you best succeed with parrots."

"Right, I take your point" — here the Director smiled — "and I won't pay too much attention to your last remark. We'll have to try it anyway and see how it goes. I'll be calling in on the primaries myself once the project's been in operation for a week or two, and I dare say a Modern Languages Inspector will be popping in now and again. Thank you for your presence, gentlemen. I'll be in touch."

Bloody typical. Yet another example, during a period of national educational crisis, of a bright and original idea fabricated by the desk-tied jackasses who felt obliged from time to time to vindicate their congenial positions in the educational scheme of things. Further, they were like staff officers who say what is to go on at the front while they themselves remain ensconced in the safety of their headquarters and are never called to account for the mistakes they make.

The primary teachers turned up, most of them tremulously and all of them reluctantly, for their lessons. Candlish, equally reluctantly — because he looked upon such a machination as merely a fancy piece of cosmetics which sounded wonderful when splashed all over the newspaper — did what he could, but without exerting himself, to bolster their confidence and to improve their diction which, if frightful at times, was no more than could be expected. He also visited them in their schools, where their performances embarrassed him as much as they did them. The Director, on the other hand, told Candlish he thought results so far were quite satisfactory and seemed disinclined to listen to Candlish's verdict, which was somewhat different. A Science teacher in his pre-administrative days, he did not know much about Modern Languages or the problems involved.

The Inspectors who came kept their opinions to themselves, for the time being at any rate. After all they had given their whole-hearted approval to this innovative gem in educational thinking and had played a leading part in its implementation. But primary teachers, increasingly aware of their inability to teach a subject which should not have appeared on their timetables in the first place, became even less enthusiastic than they had been initially and the attitude of some soon bordered on recalcitrance. Eventually many tape-recorders and wall charts and other expensive paraphernalia were surreptitiously hidden away in cupboards and their existence conveniently forgotten. After a year or two the Inspectorate quietly announced that French in the Primary School had not been a success, and it died an early death.

Yet, lo and behold, it was to be resurrected in the early nineties, with German sometimes available as well: new cassette recorders, new cassettes, new everything, and entrusted to a new generation of primary teachers who already had enough to contend with by way of curricular changes and all the added burdens foisted upon them; and it was resurrected, not in an age of abundant material resources as on the first occasion, but in one of drastic all-round cuts in the teaching force, in teaching materials, in school building maintenance. Its fate remains to be seen, but definitely no prizes for a correct forecast of the repeat of a **primary** error.

Once again, and for the umpteenth time, those responsible for learning showed themselves to be innately incapable of learning themselves ...

Chapter 10
A NICHE FOR EVERYONE

The Rector came to see Candlish one morning during one of the latter's non-teaching periods — Candlish detested the usual term "free period" since with him, and others, it was anything but that; "free" was valid only in so far as it meant "free of a class". It certainly wasn't meant to be taken literally as a synonym for putting your feet up in the staffroom, which seemed to be how it was interpreted by many. Yet they probably had a legitimate excuse, considering their exhausted state.

"Good morning! Sorry to interrupt you, Iain, but I must have a word. This will please you! The latest directive from above asks that we tap the latent talents of those who honour us with their daily presence if with nothing else. "Recreational Education" is the latest panacea. Apparently each and every one of them has his little niche and it is up to us to find it and foster it."

"You're right, I don't like the sound of it. Good Lord, are we not burdened enough as it is trying to cope with shortage of staff in the subjects we are supposed to teach?"

"I agree. But you know that rectors have less and less say in running their own schools. We're little more than rubber stamps and are expected to make our teachers act like bloody nursemaids. As I see it, this is an attempt to get the unteachable interested in something that might help to keep them out of mischief, especially when they are older and join the ranks of the unemployed. But we'll have to co-operate until they think up something else. I've already spoken to one or two of the staff who might have something to offer — John Martin says he will have a go at motorbike maintenance and Bob Smith has promised to do local walks. Peter ..."

"Local walks? My God! And with that lot? I hope he puts them on a long leash!"

"Yes, but we mustn't laugh, not too openly anyway. Peter Pressley has agreed to do canary-brooding, Harry Russel dog-training, and someone else fish-keeping. And talking of fish, I am wondering if you are willing to lay on a course in angling. You would be able to use some of your French Studies periods and also to take them out on the river now and again, I dare say."

"Now that gives me an idea. There are some fast streams and deep pools down there ideal for a certain purpose!"

"Ah, yes, but seriously, will you give it a try?"

"All right, but you know my feelings about this sort of thing and I shall do it only under protest. I'm a French and German teacher, not a bloody fishing instructor."

"*Touché,* but I'm grateful for your co-operation. You'll get some money to buy small items of equipment you might need. Rods and reels they'll have to get for themselves somehow if they don't have them. Don't use your own."

As if he needed to be told that.

*   *   *

Those who thought they were interested in the gentle art (and others who weren't) choked with excitement on hearing the news and suffered bouts of breathlessness as they spread it around:

"We're tae get fishin' fae Caundlish! He's gaun tae learn us hoo tae catch troots an' salmon!"

Up to high doh as only they and their like could be when about to embark on something — anything — new, they arrived (one of them already arrayed in an ancient pair of waders whose multi-coloured patches concealed most of the original material and another wearing a sou'wester about 10 sizes too big) outside Candlish's room with their distinctive raucous roar and as usual carried all before them, just like the River Tilloch which was then coming down in full spate and so far blissfully unaware of what was being planned to befall its attractive waters and its normally peaceful banks.

But first of all Candlish had to endeavour — endeavour being all too much the operative word — to give them some basic and very simple instruction in the classroom. He decided, in the first instance at least, to restrict them to worm fishing, one of the more straightforward methods which demanded no great degree of skill (although its aficionados would no doubt disagree). He told them that many reliable items of the type of tackle required could be made quickly and very cheaply at home, and that this was particularly the case where worming was concerned. Open mouths and blank stares, followed by the inevitable scratching of various parts of their anatomy, did not augur too well for their piscatorial futures and the possibility of graduating to the delicate art of casting a fly. So that they could see what he was doing he used a length of thick, white string in place of thin nylon monofilament and a three-inch long piece of stout wire which he had bent into the shape of a hook with a large "eye" at the bottom; he then demonstrated the simple knot required to attach this to the string, then how to tie a loop on the other and to join it to the fishing line. He repeated the manoeuvre over and over again, by which time a monkey could have done it with both eyes shut and one paw behind its back.

Now for the test. He issued each of them with a three-foot length of nylon and a hook, quite a large one to try to make allowances for their lack of dexterity, if they had any at all, told them to get on with it and to bring the finished articles out to him for inspection.

Shrieks and howls and curses when the sharp points of hooks pricked grubby fingers; curses too when the attempted knot all fell apart and took them, after all their tribulations, back to where they had started.

"Aw, fuck this!" he heard.

"Aye, fuck it. S'no' nae fun this."

"If this is whut ye've tae dae A'm gonnae change tae the canaries."

"Aye, ye widnae get yer fingers jugged."

"Ye could so. The canary could peck ye."

Grim looks in Candlish's direction. This fishing lark was not rising to expectations.

"Oh, come on boys. Bring them out and let me see them."

No-one came.

Then someone did:

"A cannae dae it sur. You dae it fur me."

Reluctantly he did, which established the pattern, and he ended up "daein it" for the lot of them. Not what you could call an auspicious beginning; and the river with its pitfalls had yet to come.

Candlish hardly considered it worth the bother, but even so went on to tell them about the sort of spots where worm fishing was most rewarding; he drew illustrative diagrams on the blackboard, but explained that tuition would be more profitable during a visit to the river (he had obtained permission from the local Angling Club to take them on to its beat of the Tilloch) which would take place the following week. Resounding cheers. They were to bring along any rods and reels they could get their hands on, but not in the way they understood the phrase: borrowed, if need be, from anyone daft enough to entrust them with items of their gear. So they pestered any anglers they knew and managed for the most part to equip themselves with an assortment of twisted old greenhearts and split canes and prototype reels which, obviously unknown to their owners, might well have been collectors' pieces.

Somehow the local TV company got to know about this innovative form of education now being introduced to one of the area's schools and decided it would cause eyes and ears to pop if slotted into their magazine-type programme which following each evening's main news. They were always looking for the sensational and they reckoned they had it here. A producer telephoned the Rector, who got hold of Candlish, and everything was arranged.

Class RE/A (Recreational Education/Angling) were euphoric; they would no longer be nonentities, they would be world famous, they already entertained dreams of stardom. No saying what the future might bring.

Passers-by slowed in their tracks to gape at the fleet of vehicles disgorging cameras and cameramen, sound equipment and sound engineers, and goodness only knows what and who else; and ceased to be passers-by as they halted and gaped again when Class RE/A came marching into sight, their rods shouldered as if they were pikestaffs and they themselves making enough din to have all the fish for miles around scuttling off to the sanctuary of safer waters.

"They must be makin' a new version o' Ben Hur!" quipped one of the swelling band of bystanders.

"More like Dad's Army — oh no, look, they're a bunch o' young laddies."

"What the heck's goin' on?"

On reaching the swing-gate which gave access to the river the members of Class RE/A, true to form, all tried to squeeze through the narrow opening at the same time and got nowhere. Candlish, wondering why he had ever agreed to be part of this predictable pantomime, had to sort them out; nothing new in that, of course; they were always having to be sorted out.

At last they were assembled at the intended scene of operations where the TV team, accustomed to recording such pulsating events as a senior ladies bowling match for some local cup or other or a Gala Queen rattling down some village street in a flower-bedecked cart, welcomed their arrival in anticipation of producing something more entertaining than the usual piffle. Yet on scrutinizing their subjects at close range they sensed a whiff of impending disaster.

The interviewer came forward.

"Mr Candlish? Good morning! This open spot will do very well. Once we get everyone settled the cameras will sweep up and down the river and then focus for a few seconds on the boys. I'll begin with a short introduction, then I'll talk to you and to some of them. Perhaps you'll be good enough to select one or two who are reasonably articulate?"

"That's a tall order," smiled Candlish. "But you'd better avoid that one with the red hair. He has a bad stutter. And the tall, lanky one next to him. I never understand a word he says."

"Oh well, we'll see how it goes. We can always edit it later."

With that he made a sign to the cameramen and raised his microphone:

"I'm standing here on the banks of the River Tilloch, just outside Glentilloch itself, and you might well ask what I'm doing here. Well, take another look!"

(At this point one of the cameras again swept slowly over Class RE/A, quiet and inhibited for once thanks to the awe-inspiring circumstances in which they found themselves).

The Interviewer continued:

"I can tell you this — I was born about 20 years too soon because things were never like this during my schooldays. These in fact are all pupils from Glentilloch High School and they are out here having a fishing lesson from one of their teachers. Here he is, Iain Candlish. Mr Candlish, have you asked to do this on your own initiative or are we witnessing an extension of education to embrace all kinds of leisure pursuits?"

Candlish had no intention of indulging in the idealistic blahblah which was no doubt expected and he decided beforehand to avail himself of the opportunity to express his reservations about the validity of projects such as this.

"No, I'm certainly not doing it on my own initiative and yes, you could describe it in those terms. The basic idea, for what it is worth, is to try to encourage non-academic pupils to take up some recreational activity. In other words it is an attempt — if you'll forgive the educationalists' jargon — to sublimate their natural and not always laudatory instincts and to guide them along paths which will be beneficial both to themselves and to society in general." His sardonic tones, he trusted, would not pass unnoticed.

"You mean to keep them out of trouble?" This chap was no novice.

"You said that, I didn't."

"I believe you've already been giving them lessons in the classroom, on tackle-making, tactics and so on. From what you've seen how many out of this lot do you think will be firmly hooked — the term seems appropriate — and develop a lifelong love of the sport?"

"Not too many, I hope. I fish this river myself!" Candlish considered it politic to accompany his words with a broad grin.

"Thank you, Mr Candlish, I can see that you're not 100% convinced that these new ideas will be successful, and I thank you for your frankness. Now let's see what the boys themselves have to say. Your name, son?"

"Sammy Snodder."

"Well, Sammy, what do you think of being let out of school to go fishing?"

"S'a right."

"Do you like fishing?"

"Naw, no' much."

"Why are you here then?"

"Ma pal's here."

The interviewer cast a perplexed look at Candlish and stepped in front of another of his protégés. This time with less enthusiasm.

"Now, what's your name?"

"Ben Burchell."

"Tell me, Ben, why are you shivering like that?"

"Slugger Thomson shoved me in."

"Into the river?"

"Aye, whaur else?"

"But why did he do that?"

"A had shoved him in."

"Why?"

"He pinched ma crisps."

"My God, any more of this and I'll be jumping in myself," muttered the interviewer.

But he would give it one final try. He wiped his forehead with a handkerchief that was already damp, and advanced, somewhat gingerly, on yet another supposedly aspiring exponent of rod and line.

"Now what are you called, young man?"

"Bert Klausmann."

"Of German extraction?"

"German whut?"

"Never mind. Tell me, Bert, are you enjoying your outing to the river?"

"Naw."

"Why not?"

"A'm starvin' o' hunger."

"What do you like to use as bait?"

"Oanythin'."

"But don't you have one or two preferences?"

"Naw, A've jist got worms."

The interviewer heaved a protracted sigh and out came his handkerchief once again.

"Phew! You know, Mr Candlish, you would get better responses from a mentally retarded nanny goat and I fully appreciate your misgivings. God knows what the people will think if and when we put this on. But on second thoughts it might be a good laugh, although that wasn't the original intention. And it's certainly different.

Thanks for your co-operation."

In fact it did come over as being rather funny, if funny, as the interviewer pointed out, was the last thing it was supposed to be; but not everyone saw it as such and the following day one or two irate viewers rang the Education Offices to complain about their taxes being squandered in such an irresponsible and frivolous manner.

They didn't know a tenth of it.

* * *

As had been anticipated by those better acquainted than the theorists with the type of pupil for whom "Recreational Education" was designed, the scheme, like so much of the stuff being implemented in this bright New Age of educational discovery and of the educational salvation of all, was doomed to failure from the outset. This was because it was based on the hopeful but erroneous assumption that the most doltish of the dolts have that little something in their make-up which, if discovered and nurtured, will pay dividends both to them as individuals and to those amongst whom they have to live. But they, the dolts, don't want to know how a motorbike works or how to maintain it, only to drive it; they don't want to know about how to train a dog or how best to look after it, only to have it; and as far as an activity like fishing was concerned, they would have had you prepare all the tackle, hook the fish and then hand them the rod. And, perhaps worst of all, they would soon tire of the motorbike and of the dog and of the fishing rod and have to be shaken out of their apathy once more to grasp just as fleetingly at something else.

Chapter 11
DEUS EX MACHINA

Close on the heels of the introduction of Comprehensive Education to Glentilloch High, there appeared on the market what was reputedly a mind-bending aid, the quintessence of the latest technology and which, according to the pundits — and to its manufacturers — was destined to revolutionise modern language teaching and therefore to be indispensable wherever these disciplines were taught; it was somewhat clinically termed a *language laboratory*.

Laboratories were as yet not quite commonplace, and the authority decided that it would add an impressive feather to its educational cap by getting in on the act and equipping one of its schools with this universally acclaimed marvel; and for some reason it was Glentilloch High School which was selected.

Arrangements were made for Candlish to spend a few days in Glasgow and Edinburgh visiting schools already in possession of the new contrivance. His instructions were to consult the Principal Teachers, weigh up the respective advantages and disadvantages of each make and to reach a decision as to which would suit Glentilloch's needs best, always bearing in mind that the most expensive was not necessarily the most desirable.

As with the majority of the forms of complex gadgety, you have to work with them for some time to be in a position to pronounce worthwhile judgement, but after his exploratory mission and the counsel received he recommended a certain type, not the most sophisticated or the most robust but, according to those who worked with it, adequate enough — provided — and this they stressed, that it was regularly serviced. In 1972 it cost £4,000.

The apparatus was duly installed in a specially sound-proofed room by the firm's engineers, who were not over-responsive to Candlish's queries vis-à-vis its operation. In fact he was surprised, and rather annoyed, to learn that the makers did not put at his disposal, even for an hour or two, someone who would explain in detail how the damned thing worked; but, as in so many transactions of this sort, their main concern was a sale, collecting their dues, and doing a permanent bunk. This meant that he and one or two of the more technically minded members of his staff were left to struggle through a complicated manual and to learn largely by trial and error the purpose of the endless array of buttons and switches, so that it took some time before they felt sufficiently confident to use it with a class. Candlish put in many after-school hours with the French *assistante* (a student of English who spent her third year of university studies in this country and who took small groups for oral practice) composing question-and-answer tapes and others which drilled the pupils in aspects of grammar.

It was a 20-booth laboratory, which meant more often than not that a class had to be split and a teacher — any teacher — found to look after those who couldn't be accommodated. This was not always possible and it often happened that they were left to fend for themselves, with the inevitable consequences.

The singular advantage of a language laboratory, it was claimed — and with some justification, at least ostensibly — was the facility whereby youngsters could have continuous oral practice with native voices asking the questions, something which could not be done in the classroom. A monitoring device enabled the teacher at the console, theoretically at any rate, to keep an eye — or rather an ear — on any individual's performance, to check that he was doing what he was supposed to be doing and not just larking about. Unfortunately his charges got wise to this when they discovered that a telltale click in their earphones indicated that they were under scrutiny. So they would "turn it on" for a minute or two until they believed the danger to be past.

At first all went quite well. For pupils the language laboratory provided an entertaining diversion and they preferred to be questioned by a nondescript recorded voice which could not castigate them as their teacher did in the classroom. But it became noticeable that the impersonal nature of the tape began to have a stultifying effect and the initial enthusiasm to wane. The toy was no longer new. Candlish considered that the apparatus could be very beneficial to Six Formers and to students in Higher Education working on their own, but doubted its value when used with 12-15 year olds. He also found that much valuable teaching time was lost, not only by the pupils who had to be left to their own devices back in the classroom, but in preparatory operations, which included the selection of the requisite material and finding it on a 7 inch reel. The language lab could be a demanding monster.

And soon things started to go frustratingly wrong, usually due to lack of maintenance. Booths would break down in the course of a lesson and those operable finally reduced to as few as 10. The manual stated explicitly that certain essential tasks, for example the cleaning of magnetic heads, be performed weekly without fail. But by whom? No-one was assigned to carry out this time-consuming chore, which at first Candlish saw to himself but finally had to give up because it became an unequal struggle. Pleas to the Rector, and passed on by him to the authority, were summarily dismissed, and on each occasion more summarily than on the one before. More and more faults occurred, more and more booths were rendered inoperable and so shambolic did the situation become that Candlish told the Rector that the language laboratory was *kaputt* in the full sense of the German term. *Kaputt* only a matter of months after its installation.

"Well, we've warned them often enough and in the circumstances there's only one thing to do: lock the door and throw away the key."

Candlish complied with the first of these suggestions, but not with the second. He could make good use of the room as storage space. And, he reflected bitterly, his Department could have made much better use of the £4,000.

Bitterly too he recalled the euphoria of less than a year before when the local press — at the authority's invitation — had published a large photograph of him sitting in command at the console with 20 rapturous pupils all jabbering away into their microphones; and beneath it a lengthy spiel extolling the virtues of this *deus ex machina* with which the local secondary school had been favoured; and although it was Glentilloch which had been chosen to lead the way the authority intended that all the others within its auspices would be similarly endowed sooner rather than later.

More bloody window-dressing, bearing in mind what had been allowed to happen; but good clean tabloid stuff.

Generally speaking the language laboratory came, was seen, but hardly conquered. Its use by those who possessed one became more and more peripheral and it was often replaced by a few simple headsets rigged up at the rear of the ordinary classroom: more efficient time-wise, far less bothersome, more trouble-free — and there if you needed them ...

Some aids, Candlish believed, had their rightful place in the teaching of modern languages, but he remained sceptical about the majority and convinced that they were often foisted upon him and his colleagues by pressure from way-out theorists and by captains of industry who were concerned more with making a pile of easy bucks than contributing to the needs of the education service. In his opinion there was still no adequate substitute for the skilful teacher with a book in one hand and a stick of chalk in the other; reactionary and old-hat maybe, but when you considered the appalling standards of general knowledge, literacy and numeracy you couldn't help but think it was time to turn the clock well and truly back by putting an end to all the fashionable gimmickry which was often as superficial as it was useless. Sadly the day seemed to be fast approaching when time-honoured books and chalk would be regarded as relics of an unenlightened educational past and appropriate only in an educational museum, if such places exist.

Chapter 12
PETER PISSPOT

The Rector sent for Candlish one morning not long before the summer holidays and told him what was apparently good news: An Honours graduate in German with Ordinary Degree French had just been appointed and would take up his post as from the beginning of the next session. The authority had grasped at him when he phoned to ask if they had any vacancies. No-one had even seen him.

"He's an ex-Army officer who worked with the Control Commission in the British Zone of Germany after his demobilisation. He stayed on there for a number of years and then did some interpreting and translation work. He says his spoken German is excellent, which I suppose it should be. He's completed one of those abbreviated training courses, and of course passed it which, as we know, doesn't mean very much. Anyway I'm not so sure about anyone coming into teaching at the age of 46. Late starters aren't so easily moulded into the job. Too set in their ways. But we'll see."

At least he could only be better than the hopelessly inadequate Mrs Edwards, who had always insisted that her scholastic timetable be drafted to fit in with her domestic one. And Candlish would have more time for other duties.

Mr Peter Hollins arrived, garbling some vague excuse for being a day late. As soon as he could find a spare half-hour Candlish explained the general set-up in his department — including the frequency of ink exercises and amount of homework — and went over his timetable with him. He was to be given the beginners' German class and would be expected to take them right through to Higher. Therefore once he had settled he must make himself thoroughly familiar with the SCE Papers. He would also have some junior French groups, all mixed ability of course, and the most capable individuals amongst them he would tutor up to "O" Grade standard, if not beyond (the days were fast disappearing when Higher classes could be entrusted to only Honours graduates). But that would depend on the quality of his French, and on other things as well.

During the first few weeks Candlish paid regular visits to Hollins' room to see how he was coping and was not too pleased with the man's performance. He was a novice, admittedly, but one of mature years, and should have been far more purposeful in his approach and more authoritative in his handling of the class. It was not a good sign, either, that he had heard raised children's voices both before entering Room 14 and almost immediately after leaving it.

He was even less pleased a little later when he noticed that his top Third Year French group (now thankfully streamed and 10 of whom had Hollins for their introduction to German) were fidgeting about before his own lesson got under way. Not like them. He then heard a whispered: "Tell him!"; whereupon one girl, obviously chosen as spokesperson, asked blushingly if she could say something about their German lessons. Candlish didn't like the sound of that, but he knew the class intimately, having taught them all from the First Year, and if there was something they had to say then it was probably better that they said it:

"Go ahead, Fiona."

"Well, sir, it's ... it's a bit awkward, but we're hardly learning anything. Mr Hollins is always telling us about Hitler and the War and ..."

"How often does this occur?"

"Oh, nearly all the time, sir. We never have anything corrected either. And when we *are* working he jumps about all over the place in the book so we don't know where we're up to. He does it with all his classes. We decided we had to tell you, sir."

Jumps all over the place in a textbook designed to progress methodically from one lesson to the next! Good God, here we go.

You get someone you think will be an asset and this is what happens. Certainly it was wise to take with a very large pinch of salt utterances of this nature which came from the lips of pupils, but this was a batch of youngsters who were keen and interested and not likely to go in for such prevarications.

Even so he made as sure as he damned well could that he had got all his facts right. Surreptitious methods in any shape or form he normally deplored, but judged them to be quite justified in this context. So on several occasions he ambled past Hollins' door and heard all he needed to hear.

He challenged him on three scores: wasting most of his teaching time by jabbering on and on about irrelevant subjects, probably satisfying to him but not to anyone else. This Hollins strongly denied. Secondly, by leaping like a crazed frog all over the textbook, an accusation which he countered with the amazing statement that by doing so he prevented his charges from becoming bored (by which time Candlish had decided that he had a lunatic on his hands); then, finally, by failing to set the written exercises as stipulated (perhaps understandable, as his pupils couldn't have written anything in any case). This also he denied.

"Right, let's see them."

"Oh, they're at home for correction."

"All of them?"

"Yes."

"Bring them in tomorrow then, the whole lot."

When the morrow came, Hollins said that he must have lost them.

"Lost them? You've lost over 100 bloody exercise books?"

That was the last straw. He reported in detail to the Rector. The Director came down and tore Hollins to pieces, with a dire warning to better his ways. An Inspector came and did the same. But all to no avail. For some reason Hollins was incorrigible, seemingly incapable of even trying to do what he was supposed to do, and continued to ramble on obsessionally about the Nazi Hierarchy, about the Wehrmacht, about the -1XSS, about the Gestapo — all of which might well merit an adventitious mention in senior German classes now and again but certainly not to the extent that they took preference over the study of the language. It was all a matter of common sense, unfortunately an asset in which Hollins was distinctly lacking. As for his French classes — all First and Second Years — they too got the German treatment, until they got fed up with it and started to create bedlam.

On one of his now far less frequent visits to Hollins' room — less frequent because there was no longer any point in wasting his time as he had obviously come up against a stone wall — Candlish noticed a couple of German Army helmets which had been attached to the wall in conspicuous positions on either side of the blackboard.

"What on earth are these for?"

"Well, bit of German history, aren't they? Help to create the right atmosphere when I'm teaching German."

"When you're teaching German?"

* * *

Candlish kept on pressing both the Rector and the Director — not that they should have needed much prodding — to award Hollins with the Order of the Boot, or perhaps more appropriately, the Jackboot, and these two gentlemen decided, not before time, that his days as a teacher of Modern Languages be terminated only a matter of months after they had started. But, worse than useless as he proved to be in that sphere, he was still a body that breathed, and so was transferred to the job of policing classes of non-Certificate pupils (not quite in keeping with the socialist-inspired doctrine which insisted, in public at least, that those of low intellect should have the most able teachers). Any other human being with a glimmer of self-respect would have objected and promised to try and get a grip of himself, but not Herr Hollins. Relieved and happy as he was to have no more to do with him, Candlish wondered how he would ever bring III German, which he himself would now have to take over, up to "O" Grade standard in less than a year. And he was galled by the thought that in his new capacity as a sort of unqualified jail warder Hollins would draw the same salary as other teachers with equivalent qualifications and length of service but who were at least trying to do the job for which they had been appointed. It was the same old story of carrying wood which was not only dead but which had never been alive at any time; the same old story, amid all the idealistic ravings of the country's politicians, of running the things that mattered in education on a rotten shoestring and resorting to every imaginable act of duplicity, even if it belonged to the realms of the unimaginable.

Being what he was, Hollins never showed the slightest discomfort when continually assailed by the uproar from his classes of rebellious louts and the thanklessness of his new daily grind never perturbed him. Anyone else with his qualifications and experience and condemned to such humiliation would have been out of that school in a flash and into the nearby Tilloch, for the only occasions on which they briefly listened to him was when he concocted fantastic tales surrounding the German soldiers' helmets. They said they had thought they were pisspots put there for the communal benefit in the event of emergency (some of them omitted the final phrase); and Peter Hollins became known to the less refined in the school as Peter Pisspot.

So he carried on in his elevated position, session after session, while his authority, little as it ever had been, waned until it was as near to nil as you could get; so when his charges started to jump out through his windows, run round the building and back in along the corridors, thumping each classroom door on the way, the Rector finally concluded that enough was enough. Yet it would appear to be more reasonable to blame the system which allowed such a person, long known as entirely unsuitable as a teacher, to remain employed for so long.

He was offered — yes *offered* — early retirement, and as an inducement his pension was enhanced for the years he had not served up to the normal pensionable age; yes, enhanced for the years he had not served, as if he had served any at all. Yet another example to illustrate that those who, financially, benefited most from "teaching" were the ones who deserved it least.

Hollins accepted; and spent much of his free time writing letters to the local press. Their main topic was the abominable state of Scottish secondary school education ...

Chapter 13
SOME MOTHERS DO 'AVE 'EM

After a period of two years the doctors could no longer remit the lethal forces which were combining to destroy Eileen and she finally succumbed. We won't dwell on the agonizing feeling of helplessness to which Candlish was subjected during his wife's illness and the traumatic disorientation he experienced once she had gone. A number of readers will be familiar with a personal cataclysm of this nature and many of those who aren't will be so sooner or later. Suffice to say for the benefit of the latter that after the passage of 12 or 15 months, during which he often descended into the deepest depths of despair and didn't really care very much what happened to him — but felt thankful that the children were as old as they were, which also allowed him to talk to them constructively about such things — he gradually, if painfully, carved out a new life for himself and regained most of his previous enthusiasm for his work and leisure pursuits. Gradually, too, he stopped shying away from acquaintances whose expressions of sympathy often embarrassed them as much as they did him. "Time heals" may be one of those time-worn platitudes irritating to the ear, especially to the ears of those to whom the very worst has happened: yet as the months rolled on he came to realise that it was as true, ironically, as life or death themselves. It had to be.

Just about three months after his loss he noticed an advertisement in the local paper for a Principal Teacher of Modern Languages. It was an all-through convent school, heavily subsidized by the local authority, an ancient building which stood on a high eminence in secluded surroundings in Abergarvie, and a mere 10 minute walk from his house. He learned that the total number of pupils, all girls from middle-class homes, was 140, with only just over 100 in the secondary section; so teaching groups were unbelievably small by state school standards.

Candlish had motored up and down from Abergarvie to Glentilloch for 18 years on a road which was becoming progressively busier, having to arrange the sharing of cars with colleagues who also had their own transport and picking up others who didn't, all to get to a 1300-strong comprehensive which was taking on more and more pupils (from small-town secondaries reduced to primaries only) with each passing year and more and more of the features of a nuthouse with each passing week; to a comprehensive where his disillusionment and his weariness grew in proportion to the increasing demands of what had become a most arduous and soul-destroying occupation as the new ideology dug deeper and deeper. He weighed up all the pros and cons and found that the former seemed to far outstrip the latter; in fact, by comparison, all the advantages offered by such a move combined to shine out like a welcoming beacon which lured him almost irresistibly towards it. True, he would drop about £1,000 per annum in salary, but that sum existed only on paper since it would be defrayed by the cessation of commuting costs; and it would also mean a much shorter day and an end to the wear and tear on human parts not so easily replaced as those required by a car; yes, he would lose some "status", but that was something which had never figured largely in his order of priorities, and did even less so now.

Admittedly the little school was regarded as something of an unknown and mysterious quantity by the few citizens of Abergarvie who ever gave it any thought, and as something of a joke by those who did. But many secondary establishments were fast entering that category in any case so, damn it, why not?

He completed an application form which asked for more information about his religious persuasion than about things he considered much more relevant in the appointment of a Principal Teacher of French and German, and allowed himself a wry smile as his mind went back to a similar experience when he had applied for Glentilloch. They were all the bloody same with their stupid bloody questions, although this time he knew it was more than a matter of going through the traditional motions. In fact he was told by a Catholic member of staff at Glentilloch that he would be received more warmly as the agnostic he was rather than as someone who kicked with the wrong foot; also that if a disciple of the faith applied, even with the reputation of being the most inept language teacher on the planet, then he wouldn't stand a chance.   First things first.

These predictions, as it happened, proved to be impertinent as far as he personally was concerned because he was the sole applicant for the post, and in such a case expediency usually won the day. The interview took place in a quaint little room dominated by an incongruously large stained glass window depicting the Virgin, at least 10 foot tall, in all her purest and benignest glory (reminiscences of Holy Horry's enthralling perorations in a similar setting in St Mary's College some decades before). Apart from himself only two others were present — the Mother Superior who was on the verge of retiring and the Principal Teacher of Classics (a misnomer because Greek was excluded) who was on the verge of stepping into her octogenarian lace-ups. Neither of them knew anything about modern languages and both considered it well-nigh heretical that Latin had been almost entirely supplanted by the main idioms of Western Europe. It was obvious to Candlish that their delight in landing someone with qualifications and experience was somewhat diminished by the existence of what they regarded as an all-important flaw in his make-up, but better to have a non-believer or as near to that as mattered than someone who habitually marched with the Orangemen or along Ibrox Way every second Saturday; moreover Candlish's neutrality, as they tended to see it, would be open to exploitation once he had imbued the beatific surroundings hitherto unknown to him. Regular glances by both interviewers at the resplendent glass icon provided them with ample proof that miracles did occur.

He would start after serving his three months' notice at Glentilloch.

* * *

Before the end of his first day he suspected that this was not a school in the established sense of the term — and that was after making allowances for all the zany goings-on and the turmoil and the declining standards that existed in secondaries everywhere — and before the end of the week he had confirmed it. The general laissez-faire attitude that prevailed, including the acceptance of girls arriving at his room ridiculously late and in dribs and drabs (and sincerely astonished when rebuked for it) led him to ask the erstwhile Principal of Classics, now the Headmaster, for a copy of the School Rules. He was told that there were none: such implements of coercion merely served to inhibit the development of individual minds and to restrict free choice. This struck him as being rather odd, since only the previous week the Big Boss himself had been ranting on again about the damning evils of contraception and abortion in any shape or form and in any circumstances.

The few books available to the Modern Languages Department, tortured and bedraggled, patched and repatched with cellotape to stave off total disintegration, and some with pages missing, bore a striking textual resemblance to the dreary Latin primers of pre-Second World War days and indeed their dates of publication confirmed their vintage. Candlish immediately got in touch with his successor at Glentilloch, George Murdoch, explained the emergency and asked if he could borrow for the time being some texts he had contemplated throwing out but had consigned to the furthest depths of the bookstore. They, too, were out of date, but still a vast improvement on what he had acquired at the Convent; Murdoch readily agreed and arrangements were made to have the books delivered to

Candlish's house by a member of the Glentilloch staff who lived in Abergarvie. For obvious reasons he kept mum about what he regarded as merely a temporary and makeshift solution when he made a further visit to Mr Marcello to ask when the next requisition was due:

"Oh, we don't have requisitions as such, Mr Candlish. If you need something desperately you consult me and I see if there are any funds available. But I emphasise that your need must be desperate."

"Well, considering that the French used in these books is almost extinct and most of it beyond the comprehension of the average living Frenchman, I would say that my need falls into that category."

"Oh, that is very strange. As far as I know Mr Docherty had no complaints about them."

By this time Candlish had learned that his predecessor, a hopeless drunk whose lunch invariably consisted of three or four pints of beer in a riverside tavern, had sometimes not even bothered to, or had been incapable of, coming back for the afternoon session. If he did return he often fell asleep over his desk, oblivious to everything while mayhem reigned all around him. Compared to him, Hollins at Glentilloch had apparently been something of a godsend — and you can't say more than that. Results in SCE exams had of course been permanently woeful during his tenure of the post and his best year (when, perhaps due to some form of divine intervention, his lunch-time intake had amounted for a spell to no more than two pints) had produced a couple of Highers and five "O" Grades from a presentation of four times that number. No doubt the Hail Marys had rung out loud and clear on that occasion.

"According to what I've heard, Mr Docherty was rarely in a fit state to know what he was using. I must have some new books right away. Otherwise I can't operate."

Mr Marcello, unaccustomed to dealing with straightforward talk and lacking the capacity to cope with it, muttered a not too convincing promise that he would see what was in the coffers. In fact Candlish got what he wanted, at least most of it, within a month. Perhaps they had passed a skullcap round the parents.

Meanwhile he had made some use of the textbooks resurrected from Glentilloch, but taught for the most part out of his head, and had to try to write essentials, including short exercises, on what must have been the prototype of the wall blackboard, one of those shiny, skitey things which didn't like chalk and sent it skating a good foot with a frenzied screech before it flew out of your hand to leave, at best, a single letter and then a long, faint scratch where the rest of the word should have been. Fortunately the board boasted a more cooperative area of some four feet square, all right for transcribing small items of information, but most of it was a real no-man's-land with all the attendant perils generally associated with such territory. So yet another complaint had to be lodged. And the answer?

"Mr Docherty had no objections to it."

Bloody hell. Mr Docherty again.

"Mr Marcello, I am not here to waste my time making silly complaints. But I simply can't function without a decent blackboard. Also, as far as I am concerned, there is no point in going on quoting Mr Docherty's views — or lack of them — on anything. In his habitual state of inebriation or semi-inebriation it is questionable whether he knew where the blackboard was. Even if he did the difficulties involved in extricating himself from his chair and the undoubted changes of course en route, possibly culminating in a head-on collision with his objective, would have invited calamity in front of a bunch of perpetually tittering girls who had probably been waiting expectantly for such a cause for hilarity. But look, I shouldn't need to go on like this over a bloody blackboard. If you don't believe me come and try it for yourself."

Candlish had enjoyed making his little speech and couldn't help but chortle over the ridiculousness of the whole situation. Best to see the funny side.

Perhaps Marcello did go and try out the blackboard, perhaps he didn't. But a morning or two later Candlish entered his room to find a replacement dug out from some cellar or other. One of those awkward easel contraptions, it was hardly the latest that technology had to offer but nevertheless an improvement as a writing surface. Any more of this and he would be a firm believer in the dictum he had already overhead on more than one occasion as he passed nuns in a corridor: "We must always thank the Lord for small mercies."

While still on the exhilarating topic of blackboards it might be in order to recount that on his very first day at the school he had not been able to find any chalk in his room — not knowing then that it would have been to little purpose anyway — and had sent a pupil to the office:

"Go and get me a box of chalk, please."

He wondered why the girl gave a wry smile, but was enlightened when she returned to him with a couple of sticks.

"What's this?"

"Your chalk, sir. And Mr Marcello told me to tell you that that's two days' ration."

He was aware that there were always world shortages of something: oil, copper, rice and so on — but chalk? Good God, half the South of England was made of the stuff.

That had been one of the first indications that teaching here was set to be quite an experience. If there was to be little writing on the blackboard there was already plenty on the wall.

*   *   *

It did not take Candlish long to discover something else — that far from being a sinecure in a reputedly civilised environment with small classes of nicely-mannered little girls, and some not so little, whose fathers and mothers were nearly all professionals or in business — he found himself confronted with a shower of spoiled bitches with respect for no-one. Stuffed to the tops of their high-class coiffures with prayer and hymn and sermon they may have been, and made to celebrate this saint's day and the next saint's day, but none of that sort of stuff appeared in any way to rub off on their general deportment; indeed their most unladylike behaviour could well have been a form of rebellion against it. Candlish reflected that discipline at Glentilloch, despite its large complement of neds, had been several times as good. One typical example out of many of the unbelievably lax state of affairs: it was not unusual for a girl to interrupt a lesson by barging into a room to consult her pal about their social plans for that evening; and if you admonished her, as Candlish did in no uncertain terms once he had regained the ability to speak on the first (and last) occasion he encountered such impertinence, she would be both astonished and indignant. Naturally Candlish was amazed that the staff put up with such abominations of conduct, of which there were many, and soon realised that it all stemmed from two sources: firstly, from the pusillanimous tactics of Marcello himself, who seemed terrified of upsetting the girls' parents and replaced any justifiable chastisement with a smiling little plea not to do it again, accompanied with a reassuring pat on the back, as if a sterner rebuke would have enraged either pater or mater. And it was this type of mild reaction which he expected — no, demanded — from the staff. The man, in short, was a recipe for disciplinary disaster. This was what had brought him to the Convent School in the first place — apparently he had started off his career in a large RC secondary in Glasgow and found he couldn't even keep order in his Latin classes — yes, small Latin classes — and became desperate to move to a much more serene and sheltered haven; this took him to what he considered an ideal retreat in Abergarvie, where he had thrived, in his own view, and languished in that of others, for 35 years.

The second reason for the farcical state of affairs was the gutlessness of the staff themselves. Just over half of them bore unmitigated allegiance to Rome, while the others wore the Protestant badge, ostensibly at any rate, or else didn't know or care what they were. But they all cared about their daily bread and butter and since the majority of them lacked the qualifications required to teach in the state system (no such restrictions here) they were quite prepared to keep their mouths firmly shut, no matter the amount of provocation, in case the dismissive cudgel fell. That, need it be said, applied in particular to those who could count without resorting to strings of beads, but each and every one of them understood that if you had a suggestion to make, no matter how reasonable, about better ways of doing things, you would be immediately branded as a rabble-rouser. Candlish had earned that epithet in record time and soon realised that his was a frustratingly lone voice in a sea of lily-livered apathy. He would have given much more than an eyetooth just to have been put in charge of the place for a month; just a playful thought, since there was less chance of that happening than of an invitation being extended to ex-members of the SS to join mourners at the Wailing Wall on an anniversary of the liberation of Auschwitz.

*   *   *

With so much emphasis placed hitherto on teaching standards it might be considered a surprising omission if nothing was said about the members of Candlish's "Department". He had had his problems at Glentilloch but nevertheless had been blessed for most of the time with what for those days was a sound nucleus (discounting Hollins when that gentleman still came under his jurisdiction) and his staff as a whole had probably functioned as well as most in those trying days of teacher shortage and teaching ineffectiveness and willy-nilly methods of recruitment which were distinguishable from those of the Press Gang only by the absence of physical compulsion.

In the Convent School his assistants numbered two, one of whom, a middle aged woman whose facial configurations were rather unfortunate and who exuded all the inherent charisma of a block of sodden teak, but plodded on in her uninspiring way and achieved something. And the other? Oh God, this isn't going to be easy. If Candlish could ever have been saddled with a greater liability than Hollins, then this was he; if anyone could have driven him to distraction even sooner than Hollins, then again this was he. And, unfortunately, a devout worshipper who was prized by Headmaster and nuns alike for that, and *that* was all that mattered. He would never be sent packing.

Angelo Rocca was an Ordinary Graduate in Italian who also took some junior French classes, but regrettably neither Italian nor French took precedence during his lessons or whatever these were supposed to be (in that respect he was probably no worse than Hollins, but wait). All Candlish heard from Room 3, separated from his by a paper-thin plaster partition (a former dormitory had been split into classrooms) was a daily series of detailed accounts of his assistant's enthralling weekend or evening outings with mother, going for a walk with mother, watching TV with mother (the only occasions on which "Miss Angie", as the girls had dubbed him, was free of the matriarchal fetters were when he was out at work — well, let's say when he was in school — and, if at home, during his visits to the toilet. At least we shall assume so). The general uproar was interspersed with squeals and shrieks of derisive delight from his bevy of 12-14 year olds who egged him on no end; all of which added up to a degree of uncontrolled and uncontrollable chaos which surely could never before have existed in any classroom anywhere in the land, and was unlikely ever to be repeated in any other. Yet no other teacher on the same floor had ever raised a whisper of complaint. "Oh, that's Angelo" was the definitive answer received by Candlish when he asked others why and how they tolerated it.

Aware of their own shortcomings, disciplinary or otherwise, even if these were on a lesser scale than Rocca's, they no doubt felt they had little more room to talk. After all, this was the Convent School and in the Convent School protests were very much taboo: that was the immutable order of things.

This, however, was going too far, far too far. Candlish, nearer the end of his tether than he had ever been, stamped into Marcello's office and demanded that Rocca be transferred, if not to another planet, then to a room as remote from his own as possible, preferably in an attic. The angry glare in his eyes, his tone of voice and his whole demeanour provided the so-called Headmaster with the clearest of signals that if he didn't comply he was going to have real trouble on his hands.

Rocca was moved; not exactly to an attic, but, unprecedentedly (they all knew there was little to fear) to a distant and unused room adjacent to the nuns' private quarters; and he was, and always would be, their little golden boy, despite the fact that theirs was a Silent Order (and his anything but a silent classroom) which seemed to apply as much to their soundless to-ing and fro-ing past his new abode as to their impotence to make use of their vocal chords; apart from during their frequent praying sessions, they never uttered a single cheep.

The depth of Rocca's naïveté in all things and his undisguised indifference to Candlish's attempts to try and sort him out were such that he, Candlish, soon came to regard the situation vis-à-vis his "assistant" as increasing momentum in the relentless tide against which this halfwit made him swim and decided the effort he was making was in no way commensurate with the success he achieved, because he achieved none at all. The bugger was incorrigible and as far as he cared he could stew in his own pathetic juice.

And he was insufferable in other ways too: in the staffroom he rattled on like a hyped-up budgerigar about everything and nothing, and made just about as much sense; one of his most annoying traits was his unsubtle inferences that those who held no ties with the Eternal City, as he always called it, and where he went every summer (with his mother), were members of a distinctly inferior breed, if not quite subhuman then a considerable way towards it. Candlish came very near to strangling him at times and he wasn't the only one.

Any description of Angelo Rocca would be quite inadequate as a means of expressing to the reader just how much of an apology for a teacher, and for a young man, he was. Suffice to end up by saying that he presented no worries for Pope John Paul on one score at least because at the age of 28 he still thought it was solely for peeing with.

* * *

We won't go into all the varied concepts of the aims of education, idealistic, pragmatic, woolly or otherwise. Candlish believed that the basic purpose of his job was to teach his subjects to the best of his ability, and that any beneficial by-products which derived from his wholehearted method of doing so or from his experience of life or from his personality, he assessed as desirable but coincidental. What he put first hardly tallied with the views of his employers, and it was a foregone conclusion that he would rebel against the inordinate amount of time whipped away from his timetable and the extra effort that had to be made in a futile effort to catch up. This was because in the Convent School he found further evidence, if he had not already known it, of the validity of the claim that in this world religion has as much to answer for as the lack of it. It was bad enough that morning assembly, supposedly of 10-15 minutes duration, invariably lasted twice as long and practically wiped out the first lesson; but when the omniscient grapevine relayed the joyful news, which it did regularly, that some itinerant priest or nun, or someone of higher standing in the hierarchy, chanced to be passing, praise be, within hailing distance of Abergarvie, and the girls were duly summoned en masse from their classes to listen to yet another long-winded discourse to which they paid about as much attention as they did to their own breathing, Candlish's patience reached a new low; and what was left of it vanished in its entirety when his Higher German group of seven candidates, who received only two double periods of instruction in the subject per week and therefore needed every minute they could get, was whisked away from him for the third time in a month; and not with so much as a "By your leave" — the door was just thrown open by a pupil who announced: "All the girls have to go to the hall."

But Marcello, confronted by a Candlish enraged as he had been on the day he had demanded Rocca's immediate expulsion from Room 3, remained totally intransigent on hearing his argument:

"I don't think you fully appreciate the ethos of this school, Mr Candlish. We believe that the spiritual aspect of the girls' education is as important as the academic subjects they study. Perhaps more so."

"That's blatantly obvious. But I would like to ask you something. If I told their parents that they were likely to fail, particularly in their Higher German, because they were not getting the time due them in the classroom, what would be their reaction?"

"Their parents realise that a school such as ours is much more than a piece of machinery for churning out certificates."

"Churning them out? Good God, you must surely be aware of the paucity of passes here compared with other schools. At Glentilloch I managed a far higher proportion of successes with large groups containing candidates with must less potential than they have here. But I hope you see my point because I'm becoming rather tired of knocking my brains out to little purpose. So..."

"You know, Mr Candlish, I have not had a single objection about this from anyone else on ..."

"Oh please, not that again. But what you say scarcely surpris me as this place does not exactly ooze with enthusiasm as far as work is concerned. And if these intrusions continue I'll be sorely tempted to adopt a similar attitude and to welcome every opportunity, as others do, to plant myself in an armchair in the staffroom. I want to make one more thing absolutely clear — it won't be my fault if most of these girls don't make the grade. I feel I should add that I get the impression that it wouldn't upset you too much in any case."

Nor did it seem to upset him that a Principal Teacher should be driven to speak to him in this fashion; Candlish hoped it might have brought home to him a realisation of his own wretched incompetence as a Head Teacher, but doubted it; you converted neither obsessed individuals nor moderated obsessive dogmas as readily as that.

He was right. Marcello merely sneered.

And the régime remained the same. So Candlish determined that he would no longer challenge their priorities; if the pupils were there he would teach them, if not ...

From now on his first concern would be his own equanimity.

*   *   *

For some time periodic whisperings had been overheard amongst the RC members of staff about the uncertain future of the Convent School. They appeared to be much better informed than the others, who had been told nothing at all.

Ever-spiralling costs in providing essential services had led the authority to put on their pruning agenda, not for the first time but now right at the head of the list, the advisability of continuing to subsidise to the tune of 75% what many claimed to be a glaring anachronism and whose handful of girls could be absorbed almost imperceptibly in the half-dozen primaries and the three large secondaries now in existence in the town. (Some added that the 1918 Education Act, which gave Roman Catholics their own schools, had long since served its purpose by according them social and political parity and that its repeal was overdue). At a crucial meeting one highly perturbed individual by the name of Pat O'Brien, sensing that catastrophe loomed large, considered the threatened closure to be outrageous since it would mean the transfer of a large number of girls to a spiritually less favourable environment and unfair exposure to what would be, in the eyes of the Catholic Church, dangerous influences. If all else failed, he said, half-jocularly, then they would have to seek divine intervention, which prompted the non-jocular remark from a councillor called McGregor that they could have intervention alright — of the terrestrial variety — since those who owned the convent possessed the wherewithal, in the shape of several acres of prime building land which surrounded it, to ensure the school's continuance for years to come; but that was not for sale. Oh no, far better that those holding the Abergarvie purse strings should bend their backs to scrape out the dregs that were left in their financial barrel than ask the Holy See to open the lid, however slightly, of its bottomless treasure chest.

"Right, let's take a vote," said the Chairman.

*   *   *

Meanwhile, in the Convent, the whisperings had been growing louder and the faces longer (except for one). Then a couple of days after the Council meeting, Marcello called the teachers together and told the girls to go and play themselves in the grounds. The only staff meetings that Candlish had ever known were those held for quarter of an hour or so on the first morning of each new session. So in an atmosphere that reeked of impending doom they all shuffled into Room 7.

Marcello, wearing an expression which, as they used to say in Scotland (perhaps some still do), had all the attributes of a "frostit neep", recounted at some length all the attempts he and his had made to at least delay the fateful day; he then announced, in caustic tones, that their pleas had fallen on godless ears; in less caustic tones, but caustic even so, that desperate last-minute appeals to the girls' parents had not been enough to persuade them to put their hands where their convictions were supposed to be. (This must have been most disquieting to those who thought they had a firmer grip).

The axe was to descend in one brutal sweep and the Convent School would close for ever at the end of the session in two months' time.

"God help us all," he muttered before making for the door.

God help them indeed, although he was thinking more of their charges, from now on condemned to an alien environment, than of the staff, most of whom were predominantly concerned with their own future. The unqualified amongst them knew they had no hope of being taken on anywhere, while those who were certificated knew their prospects were slim due to economic measures which were reducing teacher complements throughout the State system.

So, in mid-July, amidst much weeping and wailing, the great doors were slammed shut, bolted and padlocked. The nuns, who remained in their fortress, never went out anyway.

Candlish, as already hinted, neither wept nor wailed. But he did moan a bit. He moaned on receiving his magnificent redundancy payment of £800 — all that the Catholic governing body was obliged to pay because the school had been a "private" one and he had spent only four years in it. The overtures he made to his MP and others, arguing that he had spent 33 years in the classroom — and that it didn't seem to matter much, by his way of thinking, where that classroom was located — cut no ice either. £800 as redundancy for a lifetime's service, whilst semi-skilled workmen with 10 or 12 years were walking out of a big local factory with £10,000 to £15,000. The whole system was crazy, he insisted, because everyone paid for everyone else and a much more equable method of payment was overdue. Oh, he got sympathy and understanding in good doses, but all the officials he consulted were accomplished in running with the hare and hunting with the hounds and he knew they were as useless as were pointless the posts they often filled. Nor did he get any support from colleagues in a similar position. It was the same old story of teachers being treated as a race apart, an inferior one which could be relied upon to offer little resistance and to meekly accept its fate; and jejune as the comparison might be, it nevertheless reminded him of another race, also regarded as inferior, whose passive acceptance of mistreatment he had had ample opportunity to observe during his stay in Nuremberg. We all know the consequences of that attitude and it seemed to him that teachers were equally adept at digging their own professional graves.

Right, he decided, bugger the lot of them. At least he was still reasonably young in those days of longevity and fit enough to enjoy himself. His retirement pension, although not of such proportions as to provide for exotic pursuits or riotous living, would be adequate for his needs, and more so when significantly reinforced by his state pension and the interest he would realise from the profit made by selling his house, now far too big for him with the children gone, and buying a smaller one. But he would make sure that the smaller one was big enough for two. Just in case...

Partir, c'est mourir un peu ... He had always liked the subtly worded French phrase and had found it generally valid: St Andrews, RAF, Nuremberg (on his *first* visit), St Andrews again, Abergarvie Academy and, to a certain extent, Glentilloch High. But not on this occasion.

And he hoped he would keep on drawing those pensions until he was about 120, by which time he might have just about recouped what, by his reckoning, they owed him anyway.

Chapter 14
ENGLISH DOWN THE TUBE

In the 80s and 90s, owing to what the government blandly termed essential cuts in all branches of public expenditure, which included the depletion of the teaching force, offers of early retirement — sometimes *very* early retirement — became commonplace. The opportunity was gratefully grasped (especially by those who could remember what had been, relatively if not absolutely, the halcyon days of yore) almost to a man — or woman — as if their lives depended on it, which in certain cases they probably did. The wheel had turned full circle, creating a state of affairs which contrasted vividly with that period of dire shortage, not so long gone, when 65-year olds had been cajoled into staying on until they reached a tottering 70 and unashamed efforts made to coax back those on the verge of becoming septuagenarians: out of harness, out of touch, out of mothballs; a period during which no-one would have been surprised to hear the unmistakeable sound of a zimmer in the corridors as it supported some half-impoverished geriatric on his reluctant way to what for him would be an experience far more trying than it was for colleagues of later vintage and still in the field; hence his stay was unfailingly of short duration.

Now circumstances had been reversed and most of the early departed wrapped themselves up in their own little cosy cocoons, finding they had now both more time and energy for their bowls or their bridge or their books. Some were merely rapturous over their unexpected release and wallowed in their Shangri-la like pigs in the accumulation of months.

Yet soon the novelty, as is the case with all novelties, gradually lost its initial attraction, and a number of them began to miss the intellectual intercourse which everyday contact with their former associates had provided. Teachers, including ex-teachers, perhaps more than the members of any other profession, display an innate tendency to talk shop, and many a wife (or husband) will testify that they do it while asleep in their beds at night, probably because they are too exhausted physically and mentally to be capable of doing anything else; or maybe simply because they are so used to exercising their vocal chords in classroom instruction and staffroom polemics that the habit has become permanent and incurable.

So it came about that following an incidental meeting of a few of them in one of Abergarvie's quieter and more up-market hostelries, one of their number suggested that it might not be too bad an idea to form a sort of informal debating society to be held on an arranged evening each week. The outcome was a regular Thursday get-together at which a dozen or so usually turned up to discuss how to put education to rights, and indeed the whole world while they were at it. Some considered themselves unfortunate in not having been born half a century sooner; others couldn't quite make up their minds on this point and one, the eternally pessimistic Colin Rattray, gave the impression that he thought himself unfortunate in ever having been born at all, a view indelibly reflected on his surly countenance.

The group, all male, the majority of whom had been Principal Teachers of their own subject and had formed, as they should have done, the backbone of their various departments, or Principals of "Guidance" who had not formed the backbone to anything due to the impalpability of their remits (which the honest amongst them readily conceded) always retreated to a small cocktail bar at the rear of the building, shunned like the plague by regular clients when they saw that "the intelligentsia" were in session.

On one point at least they reached agreement: education was going, or rather had gone, to the dogs, and with the speed of whippets; and that only those who had been in the front line throughout their careers were fully cognizant of this brutal fact, otherwise by now the whole system would have been turned upside down and inside out.

(Even the meekest and the most sycophant of serving teachers were beginning to speak out, something they would never have done before). Yet John Major and Gillian Shephard, in the face of mounting criticism and pressure from employers and universities, slobbered on, just like their predecessors, about measures planned to bring about improvement, so-called remedies which were as indeterminate as they were unconvincing. No doubt about it, a poor little Cinderella education had always been, and a poor little Cinderella it would remain.

* * *

On arriving for one of their earlier forums they were greeted by an enthusiastic barman:

"Evenin', gentlemen! Hopefully you like the new colour scheme. Brilliant, isn't it?"

"No, laddie, it's not brilliant, it's matt."

This was pronounced in a tone of distinct disapproval by Colin Rattray, introduced above, who was an ex-Principal Teacher of English, and had been a good one, one who belonged to a vanishing school, one who had always insisted in his lessons on faultless speech and writing and had never ceased to blast the slovenly, much to the dismay of his younger assistants who considered him a hopeless pedant and therefore hopelessly outmoded. They swore that if he had had his way the SCE English examinations would still have included a question demanding analysis into named clauses of a long and complex sentence. His chief moan, a moan of obsessional proportions even to those who agreed with him, and only one moan of many was — need it be said? — the state of debauchery to which the language was being wantonly subjected.

The barman had stared at Rattray uncomprehendingly and the remark the young man had made, or rather the form in which he had expressed it, provided the catalyst for that evening's discussion.

"That's just typical, long-established words given entirely new meanings and causing confusion. Not so long ago it was *fabulous* or *fab*, now it's *brilliant* or *brill*. You have *gay* and *cool* and so on. Ugh! And as for that bloody *hopefully* which you hear so often even budgerigars are picking it up! How on earth did we manage without it before?

And take spelling. We're not supposed to stress it. Too hard on the kids. In any case there's no need, we're told, because they acquire it subconsciously through familiarity with the written word. With the written word! That theory might have had some validity when they *did* read, but unfortunately the only words a lot of them see nowadays are the profligacies perpetrated by all sorts of advertising or the titles on videos and computer games, so that every teacher worth his salt finds himself waging a continuous battle against these dissolute tendencies. And can we really blame them for their atrocious spelling when they are besieged everywhere by nightmarish concoctions such as *night lite, kwik-fit, nolidge, xception*, and all the others? Next we'll be seeing *Euro* written as *Uro*; and probably with a small letter, as this seems to be the latest craze where proper nouns and adjectives are concerned. It's enough to .... oh yes, just hold on a second ..."

Rattray took out his wallet and extracted from it a small piece of paper.

"This is an advert inserted by a car firm the other day in one of Scotland's quality dailies. I just had to cut it out. Listen to this — the initial *-en* of each verb beginning with that syllable has been replaced by a capital *N* with an apostrophe on either side of it:

"*'N'list* with us!!

'*N'gross* yourself, '*N'hance* your business, be the '*N'vy* of others. '*N'quire* about our vehicles and we will '*N'velop* you with the best monthly payments. We can '*N'able* you to '*N'joy* August 1st. Go on, '*N'liven* yourself — call us and '*N'trust* us with your order. We '*N'visage* you'll be glad you chose us.'

It might be easier if I passed it round."

"No need," said one.

"Quite clever, I suppose," said another.

"Quite clever? It's revolting. And I'll tell you something — if I was desperate for a car and that was the only garage in creation I would settle for a bike."

"Yes, *you* might. But you must admit it will bring in the customers because it's eye-catching."

"Eye-catching? Yes, in the same way as a pile of dog's dirt staring up at you from the pavement. You know, in that same paper yesterday one of its leading feature writers, who produces some good stuff, used something I have never seen before: *thusly*, which is not a word, has never been one and, I hope (or should I say *hopefully!*) will never be one. It's all enough to..."

"All right, all right, but let me say something. I know I'm not a linguist as you are, but regarding those zany spellings and changes in meaning you quoted, surely language isn't static, and never has been. And anyway a lot of these things are just temporary fads, like pony tails and jeans out at the knees."

"And just as undesirable. Temporary they may be but if they do go out of fashion it's only to make way for similar obscenities. It's the tendency that has to be halted. Of course language changes but I am referring to changes for the worse. And we've already reached the point where, due to their dearth of vocabulary and other factors, all but a few youngsters can't understand a piece of well-written English. To them everything is either *good* or *bad* (or, more likely, *brilliant* or *crap*) or it's *big* or it's *wee*. As for grammar, Christ! They have no conception of what the word means and they think syntax is the amount the Chancellor gets from each visit to a brothel. But it's hardly their fault when, as with spelling, teaching it is frowned upon. But not by me, it wasn't. Even people who should know better say *between you and I* and they use *less* with a plural noun instead of *fewer*. The word *whom* is unknown to most and double negatives abound. As far as some are concerned there are no adverbs in English — *he played terrific, I cued fantastic*. As for *yobspeak*, a repugnant term itself but perhaps appropriate because of what it represents, we have to listen to *we ain't, she come, we got beat*. And speech is becoming riddled with nonsensies such as *at this moment in time, at the end of the day, that's what it's all about*, all of which make me want to spit. *No problem!* and *there you go!* come into the same category. You would think English suffered from a paucity of vocabulary, whereas it is one of the richest tongues in existence. And as for the pandemic *you know!* I suppose most of us are guilty of that one now and again but for many it is a meaningless superfluity which comes at you in nerve-jangling profusion."

"Aren't you going a bit over the top? And anyway, you're on your hobby horse again. I thought we came here for a dialogue, not a bloody monologue." Bob McNish, ex-Physics, it must be said, had a clear analytical mind for dealing with things unequivocal but little patience for or appreciation of the niceties of things linguistic; he was in fact a perfect example of the yawning gap that universally exists between the man of science and the man of letters, a gap which the French have succeeded in filling more than most by insisting on a more comprehensive form of education — comprehensive in the original sense of the term — throughout its lycées. But let's not digress.

Yet, much to his own surprise, McNish had been quite impressed by Rattray's diatribe. He had never thought of such matters before, and continued:

"What about you, Iain? You're a linguist. Is Colin not making too much of all this? Better seize your chance before he opens the throttles again."

"I'm in complete agreement with him. But let me say that I

think that people like he and I, thanks to what was our everyday job, deplore more than most the rapidly falling standards to which he has referred. I too have my pet hates and in addition to the awful grammar and spelling I would add to his list the overworked *kick-start, right to the wire* and *down the tube*. Also *fun day* and *fun person* and ghastly items such as *microwaveable* and *unputdownable* and one I noticed the other day — *infotainment* (apparently that's something that both informs and entertains!) And all those abominable *-athons!* *Marathon* itself is a fine word with a historical derivation, and the same can be said for *pentathlon* and *decathlon*, but I draw a thick red line through vandalisms like *swimathon* and *walkathon*. How long before we have *shopathon* or *golfathon?* The *-aholics* fall into the same category. *Sportaholic? Chocaholic? Sexaholic?* How long before we are calling someone a *bedaholic?*"

"That could be ambiguous," said someone.

"Well, *fuckaholic* then! Ha, I like that." This worthy contribution was articulated amid a spray of alcoholic fumes from the refined mind of former Head of Physical Education, Ted Roger, and was accompanied by a rude gesture which certainly left no room for any ambiguity. But like most of his tribe he invariably resorted to indelicate behaviour when hopelessly out of his intellectual depth, having little else to flaunt apart form his imposing physical attributes.

"Trust a PE teacher to think up that one. All ballocks and no brains." Former History Principal Robin Adams detested all forms of sport and didn't have much time for Ted Roger either.

"No, but less flippantly," went on Candlish. "Of course there will always be a need for new words, especially in technology, and education too gets its fair share of bureaucratic jargon, most of it sheer gobbledegook. So does politics. Recently I heard Tony Blair use *casualization* and I could hardly believe my ears just yesterday when a participant in a radio discussion on marriage guidance came out with a really bobby-dazzler — *coupleness!* That even outshines *togetherness!* So if we must have innovations for God's sake let's try and give them a pleasing form. Churchill's *iron curtain* and *peaceful co-existence* and *summit* are examples which enhance the language, not the opposite. I think it was he who said that words are the only things that last for ever. Let's hope that he was wrong and that many of these absurdities die an early death. My God, if he was here now to see what is happening to his beloved English!"

"But there's nothing you can do about it."

"I think there is. What we require for a start is the existence of a body similar to the Académie Française with its members entrusted to protect the language from abuse by the media and commercial interests and to encourage all those who speak it to take a pride in their diction. This ..."

"Idealistic nonsense, I would say."

"I don't think so. This the French try to do and you have only to look at their schools to see that the native tongue is a far more important study than English is in ours. In fact I've never ceased to be astonished in France by the detailed knowledge ordinary men and women have of their grammar and their eagerness to discuss some of its intricate points. Try to talk on such a subject to people of equivalent standing in this country and they would think you were ripe for a loony bin. For most of them English, or more precisely their form of English, is no more than a handy mechanism for a crude form of communication and as long as they understand each other its quality is of no consequence. That's what we need — a vigilant watchdog armed with the teeth necessary to put the shackles on all those responsible for the decline in standards — and we've already said who they are. Those who get all steamed up over the slightest threat to the environment would be better employed if they directed their energies to the linguistic pollution which is all around them."

"What d'you think of Rangers' chances tomorrow night against that German team?" "All Ballocks and no Brains" had had more than enough for one night, which was his first, or for any night. In fact he vowed to himself there and then that he wouldn't be back. He would feel far more at home in the River Inn, where the clientèle talked about things that mattered, greeted each other with an enthusiastic "*Hi yuh!*" and separated with an equally boorish "*See yuh!*".

His decision became even more resolute when he realised that his attempts to change the subject had been ignored and had merely given Rattray the cue to come roaring back:

"Ah, yes, talking of football! There you have one of the best examples of the damage done by a shower of inarticulate clones constantly projected on TV or filling those bloody tabloids. I used to be quite interested in the game but I'm sick to death of the over-exposure of over-pampered players and gum-chewing managers, few of whom can express themselves any better than a five-year old — and of the obvious indifference of both the Football Associations and the TV bosses to this fact. Why for Christ's sake don't they compel these ever-presents to undergo a course in the rudiments of English and to try to tone down accents which are often so thick as to be unintelligible? A large percentage of the foreigners operating here are as fluent and grammatically sound in a language not their own as most of our homegrown heroes are tongue-tied in their native idiom. And some of ours come back after a long spell in Italy or France and can hardly speak a word of Italian or French. They're so bloody thick they don't even appreciate the opportunity they've been offered."

"Well, what do you expect? Any brains they've got are at the wrong end. And what's more, Colin ..."

But Rattray was in full cry once again:

"And this sickening *footballspeak* — and there's another gem in itself. It's enough to give you a doze of the gibbery-joos."

"A doze of the what? You've made that up, you hypocrite!"

"Well, it must be catching. *Getting a result* — as if a two-goal defeat was not a result, as if any game ends without a result. *Stringing a few results together, we'll take each game as it comes.* We're bombarded with these damnable clichés ad nauseum every time a player or a manager half-opens his mouth — and I mean *half-*opens it — plus, of course, all the pearls we mentioned earlier. Well, I feel even better now. Thanks for listening, gentlemen."

"No need to thank me. I stopped listening some time ago. I thought you'd all given up bloody lecturing, but obviously two of you haven't." "All Ballocks" again.

Steve Mathieson, who had spent much of his time in his art room, whether pupils were present or not, painting stereotyped Scottish landscapes which he sold to summer tourists and to anyone else whose appreciation of art left much to be desired, hadn't so far parted his lips all evening, except to imbibe frequent gulps of heavy draught interspersed with sips of undiluted whisky. By nature shy and inhibited, and painfully aware of it, he always felt he had boosted his ego a little if he managed to get in some kind of intellectual oar, and *when* he got it in depended on the speed and volume of his intake. On this particular evening, perhaps owing to the nature of the discussion, it took him longer than usual to get round to saying his piece:

"Y'know what I've just ... been thinking? Y'know, if all the ... hot air bel ... belched out by ... the teaching prof ... profession could only be channelled and stored like ... North Sea gas the supply would be enough to ... fuel the heating shys ... systems of ... every school from the Shol ... the Solway to John O'Groats."

Some stared, others tittered.

"How long did it take you to make that one up, Steve?"

And half-intoxicated as he was, the poor man blushed even so.

One or two, however, conscious of Steve's problem and more sensitive to human failings, clapped approvingly, without overdoing it.

Then the barman called: "Time, gentlemen, please."

"The bell has went," said Rattray.

Chapter 15
LADY LUCK EXPELLED

But long after Candlish had ceased to play a prominent role in the management of the national "O" Grade (it was the Board's policy to introduce new setting blood on a regular basis) and before the demise of the Convent School, he was asked to set two of the five papers which made up the written part of the French CSYS (Certificate of Sixth Year Studies, usually referred to as simply SYS) which he continued to do for the following three years. This was an examination, first offered in the sixties, whose main aim — or so it was generally believed — was to put Scottish first year university students on more equal terms with their English counterparts who were arriving in Scotland, especially at St Andrews, in large numbers, and with their "A" Levels were deemed to hold a definite advantage over the young natives who possessed only Highers. Yet paradoxically, the university entrance authorities seemed to regard good passes at Higher as a more reliable indication of academic potential than CSYS. No doubt aware of this apparent preference for the English qualification a considerable number of independent schools in Scotland continue to make presentations for "A" Level instead of, or in addition to, CSYS.

The techniques practised in the operation of this post-Higher examination differed in some important aspects from those which applied to Higher and "O" Grade and Standard. This was mainly due to the relatively small number of candidates, which in French total some 800-900 each year. Consequently only four or five markers were required for each paper, including Candlish as setter, while he and the Principal Examiner CSYS were responsible for the processing of marks and decided on the gradings. With only a handful of experienced and vetted markers involved it goes without saying that the Markers' Meeting proceeded quietly and smoothly with none of the ructions which could disrupt Higher and Standard and leave those present unsure of some of the decisions taken; moreover, there was little likelihood of marking inconsistency or of correction faulty enough to require more than minor adjustment.

Once the marks for all five individual papers and the Oral were printed out, showing each candidate's aggregate, some time was spent on completing a delicate balancing act in order to determine the demarcation lines separating the grades. Each candidate's performance in each paper was scrutinized and various factors considered before awarding him an A,B,C, D or E (roughly 10% received an A, 20%, a B, 40% a C, 20% a D, and 10% an E). For example special emphasis was placed on the marks gained in the papers which entailed writing in the foreign language, and it was possible for someone with a total score of say 184 to receive the grade above another with 186. Standardization and Borderline Scrutiny in the Higher and Standard sense of the term, both suspect ploys as we have already noted, did not exist.

Thanks to the procedural methods employed it soon became obvious to Candlish that candidates at CSYS level came in line for more, and better, attention than those sitting Higher and Standard. By comparison Lady Luck played at most a very minor part and of course examinees had no idea that the grade they earned was in many cases a much more precise assessment of their ability than the one they had been awarded at Higher and Standard. Even taking into account the Board's honest attempts to be fair in all its examinations, the indisputable fact remains that the greater the number of candidates involved the greater the possibility of both rank injustices and undeserved favours — a state of affairs stemming directly from the dubious practices of Standardization and Borderline Scrutiny. Forgive the cliché, but even in the prosaic field of examinations Small is Beautiful.

However it is only right to point out that practicability was of the essence and that the methods the Board adopted were to a large extent dictated by the amount of time available (examiners were frequently obliged to continue work until late at night so as not to fall behind schedule) and time was something of which it had no surplus. For a variety of reasons, and in the case of Higher and CSYS mainly to enable intending students to make timeous application for their entry to centres of Higher Education, all candidates had at that time to be in possession of their results on the same date in July, a date which was determined by those subjects involving massive numbers and hence the daunting amount of correction and mark processing entailed. ** Candlish concluded that the system designed for CSYS could, all things considered, claim to be as efficient a piece of machinery as it was possible to devise for the handling of any external examination.

No small praise coming from such as him.

* * *

Every Scottish school (and any other educational establishment presenting candidates in a modern foreign language) is obliged to send to the Board, well before the written examinations commence, an Oral Proficiency mark for each examinee.

At Standard and Higher Grade the tests are conducted by members of the school's Modern Languages Department, but under the guidance and supervision of a trained Monitor. In addition some centres are selected for the testing of a number of presentees by an External Examiner from the Board and their names are not known until that person arrives on the premises — both of these wise measures designed to deter teachers from awarding inflated marks, something which happened all too frequently before such precautions were introduced. In fact traditionally the Board has always been

---

** For many years the number of SCE *presentations* has been showing a general increase. In 1995 the figure for Standard Grade was 490,112: for Higher 160,925 and for CSYS 11,900: a total of almost 663,000. The total number of *candidates* was just over 124,000.

wary of accepting any kind of internal assessment and only in fairly recent years has the oral mark been included in the candidate's aggregate for the whole examination.

At CSYS level, however, each examinee has to undergo an official Oral Proficiency Test conducted by the Board. And on his retirement from teaching Candlish received yet another invitation from Dalkeith, this time to act as External Examiner for CSYS French, one of a team of half-a-dozen who would conduct the entire operation out there in the field.

He did not even hesitate. This would make an interesting change from setting written papers and provide an opportunity to remain involved in education and to gain an insight into this aspect of the SCE. He began to think that the Board must approve of him.

So he went to Dalkeith and spent the greater part of a day with his colleagues listening to and discussing and evaluating a selection of candidates' answers on tape. All the oral tests had to be completed during the last week of February and the middle of March and a great amount of preliminary spadework had to be done both by the Board and by himself, his own share of it arriving in the shape of a bulky folder containing much information and several different types of forms: there was a list of the schools allocated to him — 44 in his first year, which was really pushing things a bit — with their addresses and telephone numbers and the dates which, for one reason or another, were unsuitable for his visit; these included school holidays, days on which internal examinations were being held or on which CSYS candidates would be absent (perhaps having an "open day" at a university) so while working out his timetable he had to keep his eye on a multitude of factors. Everything in the jigsaw had to fit.

He sat down with large-scale maps of Scotland and of Glasgow (Edinburgh did not figure in his itinerary) and proceeded to arrange the schools into clusters: Hawick High, Jedburgh Grammar, Selkirk High and Galashiels Academy could, for instance, be completed in a single day as long as the groups in each consisted of no more than three or four candidates. It was much easier to calculate travelling time in an area like the Borders than say, in the Central Belt, yet it was always wise to allow for road hold-ups and also for snow and ice. Once he had planned his programme he entered the details of his proposed visit in a pre-typed letter provided by the Board and sent them all off to the Rectors concerned.

Fortunately nearly all the replies were in the positive but clusters were spoiled by those that weren't; in such cases Candlish soon learned that it entailed less trouble for everyone, and above all for himself, if he did not suggest a revised date for those schools which had already accepted his arrangements — you could be almost certain that at least one of them would say the new one was inconvenient; far better to let things be and attend to the handful of "rogue schools", as he called them, at the end of the period when all the others were out of the way.

Finding schools in country towns, where many of them were, presented no problems, but he encountered difficulties in Glasgow and in "new towns" of which East Kilbride and Cumbernauld were the primary examples. In the former there seemed to be only dual carriageways and although he could often identify his target on the "wrong" side of the road, access to it could be ridiculously complicated. As far as he could make out East Kilbride possessed no traffic lights, and in their stead roundabouts here, there, and everywhere — small wonder it bore the sobriquet "the polo mint town". Cumbernauld was even worse, with no rhyme or reason to its layout and with no-one around who could be asked for directions. Not being too familiar with routes in Glasgow and after becoming quite disorientated on more than one occasion he finally resorted to taxis and suburban trains; otherwise he was likely to arrive at a school behind schedule owing to faulty navigation and traffic congestion.

During the four years he conducted the oral he travelled the length and breadth of Scotland and visited well in excess of one hundred different schools ranging from Stranraer to Eyemouth, from Lerwick to Stornoway and to that scenic gem called Plockton (whose classroom views are surely unsurpassed by any anywhere) and then down to Oban and to Campbelltown at the foot of the Mull of Kintyre. The number of candidates to be tested in any single school rarely exceeded ten, and while the normal figure was between two and five there was frequently only one (as in the Anderson High in Lerwick, which involved a drive to Aberdeen and a 14-hour ferry crossing). And snags did occur now and again: on arriving at Wemyss Bay one morning to get across to Rothesay a March gale kept all boats in the harbour and he had no option but to return to Abergarvie and make the journey a week later. The 20-odd schools he visited in Glasgow required five or six full days work and the contrast could not have been more marked as he moved from a teacher's paradise such as the independent Laurel Bank or Craigholme to some of those state institutions in the inner city or in the large housing schemes .

The test (15-20 minutes duration) consisted of reading aloud a passage of literary French and then answering questions on its content, further questions on topics of general interest and finally a few on the prescribed novels or plays the candidates had studied and on French history and "Civilization" (painting, history, music).

Candlish was hardly impressed by the general standard of oral proficiency at this post-Higher stage; he was not impressed because these were invariably youngsters specializing in modern languages and who had been reared, in their initial years of instruction at any rate, under a predominantly oral system. So it really was disheartening when you started off with a simple question aimed to boost the examinee's confidence — perhaps "*Quel temps fait-il aujourd'hui?*" only for him to glance at his watch and reply: "*Il est dix heures et demie*" (or something similar but grammatically incorrect). Bad pronunciation and poor intonation were widespread, as was the inability to understand fairly straightforward questions. Yet there were, mercifully, some who made the proceedings quite pleasurable by displaying, if not grammatical accuracy, a commendable degree of fluency and spontaneity, even putting in little asides and disagreeing with Candlish's opinion when questions became more abstract and searching. Responses of this nature provided welcome relief in an exercise which could be, and in many cases was, an ordeal for both parties. It came very close to being that for Candlish, but in an entirely different sense, in one school in Lanarkshire when he discovered right away that the charismatic girl sitting opposite him was someone very special, the likes of whom he would never encounter again. She answered each question effortlessly and idiomatically, with a beautiful accent, obviously in total command of the language and thoroughly enjoying herself; in fact he felt she was testing him as much as he was her. Intrigued, he asked about her background, and it transpired that her father was a Principal Teacher of French, her mother was French, and only French was spoken at home. He had no hesitation in awarding her the maximum mark of 50 — on the basis that her performance was as good as could be expected of any CSYS candidate. Hers went far beyond that.

Apart from his spells in Glasgow he estimated that he spent far more time driving or sailing than he did examining, and during his first three-week assignment he covered some 1500 miles at the wheel of his car or on ferries. As with the fees for handling the written examination these seemed to be incommensurate with all the work and responsibility involved: in the early 80s £14 per day and £7 per half-day less tax — and no recompense for all the administrative tasks carried out at home. But that was partially acceptable in view of the fact that he, as far as he knew, was at that time the sole member of the oral team without employment, all the others being college lecturers drawing their full salaries. If he didn't over-indulge himself however, he could make a moderate profit from his expenses, although these were not lavish in the first place in respect of overnight accommodation and the car rate per mile was less generous than that paid by any other body with which he was acquainted — and was even halved after the first 150 miles of a journey.

Yet he was glad to get out and about and relished the continual change of environment and the conversations he had with Rectors and Principal Teachers. But, as in the case of the written examinations, there came a time when he reached a certain age and was forced to stand down; and on this occasion his severance from the Scottish Examination Board, after an almost uninterrupted association lasting for 15 years, was final.

Chapter 16
THE BUREAUCRATIC BOGEYMAN

In the latter part of the century the speed of the all-consuming avalanche of change in every conceivable, and inconceivable, aspect of school education was matched only by the intensity of the pressures imposed on teachers as they tried to cope; while their "unions", true to form and to their policy of appeasement, remonstrated only feebly against the more outrageous innovations and in the main acquiesced. Struggling to cope was, as will have been gathered, something to which those operating in the classrooms were long accustomed, something they had apparently accepted as an inherent part of the job, but now the demands went far beyond overloaded timetables, the escalating problem of indiscipline and the thousand and one frustrations that had become their daily lot.

We shall not bore the reader, assuming we are not doing that already, with all the details concerning Parent Teachers' Associations, School Boards, and Consultative Committees; with changes in syllabuses, in SCE examinations and standards, plans for new examinations and scholastic tests — often abandoned, resurrected and abandoned again — and God knows what else, not forgetting the regular stream of "pilot schemes" for which there were no navigators and with pilots who would have had difficulty in steering a wheelbarrow; and all this at a time when teaching complements were being reduced and class sizes increased, when regional education offices were being inundated with new Directors and Depute Directors and Assistant Directors for whatever you like to name — as a glance at the advertisements in the *Scotsman* or *Herald* on any appropriate day will reveal — all of them alarmingly reminiscent of the vaguely-designated sinecures already existing in the "Welfare Services", of which education seemed to have become a close ally if not an integral part; and all of them supported by legions of somewhat lesser mortals, all of them engaged in perpetrating every plausible or downright implausible activity and in so doing qualifying for very respectable salaries and allowances, thereby depleting the coffers of funds which could have been assigned to fundamental ends; and this *menage à tous* running berserk when schools all over Scotland, many of them built on a "functional basis" in the sixties, were falling into a state of disrepair: leaking roofs, heating systems that were continually breaking down, books and equipment ruined by dampness. In 1995 £500m was urgently required to put matters right. But how much was allotted? £70m. One or two examples: Highland Regional Council alone needed £34m to redress defects at Fortrose Academy, at Lochaber, Glen Urquhart, Portree and Ullapool High Schools, to name only the worst and to exclude primaries, but were allowed to spend a mere £3.2m and, despite vigorous campaigns by indignant parents, were forbidden to borrow a single penny. At Ullapool most of the lessons took place in 20 "temporary" cabin classrooms, while Portree came second with 16. When all these factors are taken into account it is hardly surprising that teachers who had been models of conscientiousness and competence and now, through no fault of their own long past both their tether and their best, became sick to the marrow of the whole damned business and each day looked with increasing impatience for that officially-marked envelope to come flying through their letter box and to announce the best news they could be given in this the worst of all possible educational worlds.

At the end of their tether — an exaggeration? Not at all, because amidst all these goings-on or, as we have just observed, lack of the right things going on, their exasperation was finally fuelled up to exploding point by the painful realization that the stage had now been reached where one small point was being completely ignored: that the most important person in the entire education service is the teacher in the classroom, that everyone else and everything else is ancillary to him, that no-one else would be there in the first place but for him. That was how it used to be before the bastard monster was conceived in some potty pedagogical laboratory to be let loose with its ever-lengthening tentacles to strangle what a former basic administration had been there to nurture and protect. Education isn't an organization like a modern air force requiring a huge supporting staff to keep a few highly-trained fliers operational. It demands a policy exactly the opposite: better by far to have too many teachers in the schools — a distinctly remote possibility — than too many pompous parasites outside them. The situation provides as perfect an example as any of losing the sight of the wood for the trees, or of the classroom for the admin. block.

It was this bureaucratic bogeyman, a miscreation in size and concepts and a Meddling Minnie if there ever was one, which administered the final demoralising factor as far as already overburdened teaching staffs were concerned. Some of its victims just couldn't handle, or ultimately refused to handle, the endless and multifarious communications about this, that, and the next thing, often as ethereal as they were inconsequential; and a mere glance at the title of the latest directive, which probably contradicted an earlier version, was generally enough for it to be consigned, with a prolonged sigh or an impatient oath, to where it rightly belonged; in fact so conceited and naïve did the authors of all this trash show themselves to be that it never occurred to them that just as verbosity, sooner or later, falls on deaf ears, an immoderate indulgence in written jargon merely results in eyes that do not see. Never before, surely, in the whole wide range of human activity, have so many little twits conspired to churn out so much mumbo jumbo to the benefit of no-one and to the detriment of all — themselves excluded, of course, smugly comfortable as they were in their gravy train which welcomed aboard more passengers with each passing year. We shall add just one more specific example: in late 1995 Socialist MP, Mrs Maria Fyfe (no relation to the writer) announced that Labour Councils would be likely to appoint an Education Committee and a Director of Education, with Chief Officers. Exciting news — for those aspiring to the posts and for the manufacturers of railway carriages.

* * *

It may be puzzling — or maybe not, in view of all that has been said — that the Scottish Office, with the cooperation of the General Teaching Council, local authorities, and the training colleges themselves, continued to accept an excessive number of recruits, knowing full well that between 1988 and 1993 an average of only two in three in both primary and secondary found a job within nine months of completing their course. In 1995 the chances were much less in primary at just over one in two, while in secondary they didn't even reach that level. In primary, 500 qualified that year from Moray House Institute in Edinburgh and Northern College (with campuses in Aberdeen and Dundee) alone but how many vacancies existed in Lothian, Grampian and Tayside? One hundred. Yet if there is any field in which staffing requirements can be forecast with almost 100% accuracy, then that field is teaching, since pupil intakes into primary and secondary are known five or 12 years ahead respectively. Is there no recourse to birth rate figures in a place like the Scottish Office? Even if the plan was to get rid of experienced teachers at the top of the salary scales and to replace them with cheaper novices at the bottom (hardly a recipe to promote higher standards) the extent of the miscalculation remains incredible.

* * *

The question might well be asked: Why, if teaching appeared less than attractive by the absence of decent salaries (at least those paid to well-qualified specialists in secondary schools), status in the community and support from those above, did so many young men and women apply for training? After all, senior pupils in particular could see daily what went on around them but shouldn't have, and what didn't go on and should have; and if there was one vocation about which they knew substantially more than they did about any other, with the possible exception of that of father or mother, it was teaching. So most of those with a modicum of common sense and self-esteem refused pointblank to put it anywhere on their list of preferences; if they did, it came right at the bottom and probably in brackets.

Throughout his career Candlish had known of no efficient teacher who had ever encouraged any of his pupils to enter the profession, but knew of several who had done the exact opposite, and of some who had just fallen short of disowning their own children, especially if they were males, if they seriously entertained taking such a step.

One or two applicants, a very small percentage, belonged to that category who genuinely felt, in spite of all the warning lights, that they wanted to become teachers more than anything else; others held qualifications not good enough for, or unsuited to, the traditionally desirable professions or promising openings in commerce or industry, and their main concern was to find employment of some sort, even if it had to be in teaching — they could always keep their eyes open for something better to come along; then you had those who provided all the proof that was needed of the old adage: "Those who can't, teach"; and teach they couldn't because the attributes required they did not possess. As arch plitterers by nature they were totally incapable of any degree of self-discipline, capable only of monkeying about — we have already met one or two — with no intention of applying themselves to the hard graft of classroom instruction but with every intention of engaging in all sorts of frivolous pursuits such as a Brownie leader might perform. One of them in any school is one far too many and sadly there are far more than that. Barring the introduction of a rigorous system of recruitment and an equally rigorous monitoring of beginners, with the merciless expulsion of all failures, schools will continue to harbour these third-rate misfits and to do at best a second-rate job. No business enterprise would ever survive if it carried such baggage. Accountability on the one hand, none on the other. Schools run by the government are not in the business of making money; those in the private sector are, and we all know the extent of the scholastic gulf that separates the two, and why. The fact that the lesser-known private institutions don't usually aspire to the achievements of the most élite does nothing to weaken the argument; they simply charge less and pay less, and because they pay less ...

Towards the end of 1995, following a survey by HM Inspectors, it was disclosed that England and Wales employed 15,000 teachers whose performance was so bad that they ought to be given the immediate order of the boot. On a pro rata basis, and other things being equal, which admittedly they seldom are but in this case equal enough, this would mean that Scotland should get rid of some 1500; and these would be only the worst of the worst and would exclude two or three times that number whose marginally better contribution is still so bad as to have them too classified, realistically, as not so much of doubtful worth as of undoubted worthlessness.

It has often been suggested that "payment by results" would be the answer, but this would entail a method riddled with difficulties, too obvious to mention. No, the best solution, the only feasible solution, is the one just suggested: accept only the most promising, and confirm over a period that their promise has been fulfilled. If not, bring down the axe. It can be done, and it must be done.

At this point it is interesting to note that in 1995 the UK spent £35b on education, an apparently huge sum but exceeded by the budgets for local government and social welfare; in France, on the other hand, the teaching of the young cost more than anything else. Perhaps that explains that whereas 7% of British children attend private schools (and the figure is growing) the number doing so in

France is infinitesimal. French parents are quite satisfied with their state system and even the well-heeled see no need to send their sons and daughters to fee-paying institutions. This includes their socialist politicians who, unlike others who have come to our notice, share the same opinion. But then again France values her teachers not as child-minders but for their ability to teach, and ensures that she gets those who can. As in several other European countries this is achieved by offering salaries — and hence a status — much superior to what we have here.

Trite remark or not, what you get depends largely on what you are willing to pay. So if all you can rise to is leftovers from the administrative table ...

Chapter 17
SITTING ON THE PERENNIAL FENCE

Candlish enjoyed his retirement. He enjoyed it because unlike many unfortunates whose working life had been exactly that and little else, and who didn't know how to occupy themselves once freed of the vocational shackles — finding something to do "to pass the time" is always a sad state of affairs — he welcomed the opportunity to indulge to the full in his favourite pastimes. Yet total retirement did not come right away: as we have seen he carried on for a spell until the Examination Board, in accordance with their rules concerning age limits, politely severed a long mutual relationship, first as setter, then as oral examiner. But he still found adequate intellectual outlets in writing articles for angling magazines and on diverse subjects for newspapers; he took on private pupils, as much for the sake of keeping up his French and German as for financial gain; he fished a lot, read avidly and visited the Continent most summers and sometimes in winter. He did have the occasional liaison with a member of the opposite sex, and in that sphere too, his tastes were as discerning as they were in everything else: the lady had to be well-groomed, articulate, fairly knowledgeable, and definitely no chatterbox; and not interested primarily, if at all, in the antics of the Royal Family, TV soaps or TV chat shows. There were not too many in Abergarvie and its environs who filled this demanding bill, and those who did apparently remained hidden away and difficult to track down. Still he managed ... At one stage he even toyed with the idea of remarrying, but thought better of it. Why bother? A periodic affair, if only of a few months duration (after which it usually palled, he himself usually being the guilty one) was all that was needed, and it was safer. Best of both worlds, perhaps. Yet he never completely discarded the possibility of further wedlock. He realised he might change his mind as the inevitability of increasing immobility and loneliness came with increasing age. Selfish bastards, men.

He also reflected a lot. While in harness as severe a critic as any of what he saw as a rapidly deteriorating state educational system, he could now review it in retrospect and, he trusted, impartially. But Candlish had never been one to destroy something just because it was destructible: its destruction had to be desirable. Any idiot could demolish, but if you did so you had a moral obligation to suggest ideas for reconstruction. Perhaps, paradoxically, the bigger the mess, the more straightforward the task. The whole rotten structure had to be stripped to its foundations: no more patching up, no more ersatz materials, no more meaningless blahblah from those in charge. Only meaningful action would suffice.

The shortcomings, in Candlish's opinion, were manifold, but there were three which were basic and dwarfed all others. Two of these, low teaching standards and the predominance of too many cooks in their ivory kitchens churning out recipes injurious to the well-being of both teachers and taught, we have already examined in some detail. But since the much too high incidence of poor teaching performance is in the main the end result of generally poor salaries it might be interesting to look at some salient points with regard to what various grades of teachers are paid. We shall then investigate the third, the ogre of indiscipline and its bedfellow, truancy.

Since the end of World War Two the Educational Institute of Scotland, with practically every one of the great multitude of primary teachers a member, has been guilty of a form of nepotism by confining its efforts to looking after its own and dear, even if this disadvantages, salary-wise and status-wise, those with higher academic qualifications but outwith its fold. This was the attitude of an institution which, as already stated, claimed to be dedicated to the furtherance of all learning throughout the land. With its Executive dominated by primary or ex-primary staff it had, well before the close of the century, achieved its major aim by persuading the government to reduce to a single common scale the nine which for so long had recognised, and catered for, the huge variations in scholastic attainment which existed in the profession. The primary teacher, who had no specialized knowledge of anything, and the secondary teacher, who had specialized, say in Mathematics or English, were all comprehensively lumped together and, just like their pupils, considered to be of equal worth. The financial cake remained the same in size — which was all that seemed to matter to the Treasury — but was cut up into equal slices. The sole concessions made to graduates were so trivial and derisory as to make one wonder why they were made at all (and could be interpreted only as a contemptible sop suggested by some whose consciences were not entirely guilt-free): Ordinary Graduates would start at the second point on the scale (at the moment of writing £12,147-£20,190 per annum) and Honours Graduates on the third. Compare this with the situation in 1968, for instance, when the nine scales were operating and an Honours Graduate earned from £1020-£1980 and a Primary non-graduate from £640-£1040. What did this incongruity signify? It signified Dilution; it meant that after 10 years service an unpromoted primary teacher who had held the minimum qualifications for entry to training (three Highers and two Standards) and had undergone a relatively undemanding programme of studies thereafter, received exactly the same remuneration as an unpromoted First or Second Class Honours Graduate in a secondary school.

But not only the Educational Institute of Scotland merits unreserved censure for the part it played in creating such an outrageous anomaly: blame, and plenty of it, must be apportioned to the Scottish Secondary Teachers' Association, supposedly in existence to act as a bastion for the protection of its rank and file against such machinations engineered by the rival camp. It objected, of course, but in its usual wobbly-kneed manner — and was simply brushed aside. Its failure to obviate a calamity of this nature (and we refer not only to an unrealistic salary structure but, by implication, the likely decrease in recruitment to the secondary sector of the most highly qualified) should have sounded the death knell of this so-called "union", yet didn't; that was proof enough, if any further proof was needed, that the degree of submission of its executive was matched only by the unassertiveness of its members. Had they had any spirit at all they would have done whatever was necessary to have such an aberration quashed as soon as it was first mooted.

In accordance with the modern hocus-pocus that upgrades designations in jobs that have not changed one whit (a Housing Factor is now a "Director of Housing" and a dustbin man an "Environmental Officer", while organizers of the rugby scene are "Directors" and football commentators have become football "Analysts") the young primary teacher no longer receives a mere Diploma on completion of her course: since 1984 she has been ceremoniously invested with the new Degree of Bachelor of Education. Of course, as in the examples given above, you can call anything what you like if you think it makes it sound better; to all intents and purposes this was merely a different piece of paper testifying to the same rudimentary knowledge of a variety of general subjects and assuredly no more a criterion of intellect than the former piece of paper had been.   In fact secondary staff were known to shiver with trepidation as they recalled the calibre of some of the pupils in V and VI who had sailed through their B.Ed. and then been let loose on unsuspecting juniors; you just shouldn't be teaching English if your own is sadly lacking in grammatical accuracy and vocabulary and you shouldn't be teaching numeracy if you need a calculator to top up a simple bill; nor History or Geography if your basic knowledge of these subjects is obviously flawed. It could be truthfully said, as far as formal qualifications are concerned, that there are in existence today a far from negligible number of primary teachers who are by no means underpaid.

In 1995 the sole teacher (with the grandiose title of "Head") of a primary school somewhere in the hills with 14 pupils was receiving a salary of £25,608, while an unpromoted Honours Graduate in a large city secondary, with classes of 30+ and responsible for advanced work with SCE candidates, was estimated to be worth £5418 a year less. A primary Head with 460 pupils and a staff of 17 was paid £32,505 while the Rector of a secondary with the same number of pupils and 38 staff earned £36,492. Further, a secondary school embraces three taxing and time-consuming areas, two of which do not exist at all in an elementary establishment, and the third only to a much less significant degree: the intricacies of timetabling (and the need for constant retimetabling), the endless paperwork and organization involved in SCE presentation, and the maintenance of discipline. Primary youngsters, as we shall soon see if we don't know it already, are not all fashioned in the cherubic mould, but who would not rather be faced with a few obstreperous 5-12 year-olds than hordes of rebellious teenage louts, especially those in the 14-16 age bracket? Yet the large primaries boast not only Depute Heads, but even Assistant Heads. What do they all do? If secondary schools are overloaded with non-teaching or part-teaching administrators, as we have already observed, then God knows what terms would be appropriate to describe the situation in their junior equivalents. And no doubt the EIS, the biggest Diluter of all, has had a fair say in this too.

*   *   *

Teaching stands as the sole vocation which presupposes an essential ingredient without which its efficacy is sorely reduced or completely wanting — the maintenance of a type of discipline which has no parallel elsewhere. In that it is unique. When only some measure of this ingredient is present the machinery of classroom instruction splutters and falters; with hardly any of it, or none of it at all, that same machinery grinds to a halt and all production with it.

Teaching expertise, a profound knowledge of the subject, a high degree of articulation, an ardent desire to succeed, all of these count for nothing if a teacher cannot make his voice heard amidst the uproar around him. The man in the room next door, less generously endowed with the aforementioned skills, but with the ability to keep order, will achieve much more than he, who will achieve precious little or nothing at all. How can he, when all his energies are directed towards screaming at those in front of him, beseeching them to be quiet? Or if he simply capitulates, lets them get on with it, and at least spares his vocal chords? And this from the moment the lesson begins until it ends. He fights a battle which has been lost before it has even started, and all because his armoury lacks the weapon which matters most, that elusive quality in a teacher which ensures that pupils sit up and listen and do as they are told.

Eternally puzzling it is that those unfortunates who cannot keep order (bearing in mind that in an earlier age the least feeble amongst them would have had few difficulties) can go on suffering such ignominy — and torture, since a form of torture it undoubtedly is — day after day, week after week, and even incredibly as we have already seen, year after year. Of course many of them don't; they fall ill and by the wayside ... and eventually disappear. Yet amongst them there are others who, unhappily, have the propensity — if that term is appropriate — to put up with this sort of living hell without visual scars to either body or soul. To them it is dismissed like water off a whale's back, and no matter how often the monster surfaces the water continues to run.

It should be stressed that we are talking of extreme cases, and mainly where teachers are involved with pupils of low ability. At the same time tumult on this scale also exists in certificate classes, particularly in younger classes of mixed ability which contain certificate pupils. You hardly expect it, and rarely get it, in independent schools, with their selective intakes, smaller classes, and parental support; it is also less of a problem in small rural comprehensives, although there are exceptions. It is in the others, in the towns and cities, with their rolls of 500 to 1000+, that the worst examples occur.

We have said that teaching, as a job, is unique. No other in creation, for its successful fulfilment, depends upon the successful establishment of the total dominion of one adult over 30 or more lively and possibly hyperactive youngsters for several hours each day. The doctor, the lawyer, the shop assistant and the driving instructor can all feel stressed at times but they are not prevented from getting on with their work and never experience the collective and wearing type of abuse that is far too frequently, if in varying degrees, the soul-destroying and utterly demoralizing lot of a large number of teachers.

One might compare the position of the soldier who, like the scholar, has often to be taught in large groups. How could he, even if he were a conscript, ever learn his trade (and not prevent others from learning theirs) if he constantly disobeyed orders, disrupted his instructors and caused general mayhem on the parade or training ground? He would not do it because the penalties would be too severe, and if he did do it he wouldn't do so a second time. But ah, one might say, the soldier is a young man, not a child, and in any case he expects the discipline to be tough. It's different, you see, when you are dealing with children. Really? But for them, too, the penalties used to be severe — and the discipline correspondingly good. That is because it was accepted that a school, like an army, could not function properly without it. So what on earth has happened to the strict school code of not so many moons ago? What on earth has happened to bring about a situation in which even 5-year olds are creating merry hell, becoming more aggressive, more indifferent to horrendous violence, and are molesting each other sexually? In which teachers in schools in England find their desks and briefcases booby-trapped and even containing human excrement? In which "street culture" is becoming endemic and more and more pupils are coming in armed with chains and baseball bats? In which 11% carry large knives and cleavers and 4% have guns? (One female teacher risked the sack by making a video — shown on TV — of her typical day in school as she believed the public had little idea of the seriousness of the problem). Again, even in primaries, women teachers complain about the increase in the number of sexual innuendos and lewd remarks — and some pupils were going even further and trying to fondle their breasts. In all of Newcastle-upon-Tyne's 120 schools panic buttons, connected to police stations, have been installed and each teacher has been provided with a personal attack alarm. It was estimated that in 1994 around 40% of all teachers in the UK were assaulted in one way or another and that 16,000 of these attacks could be labelled as serious. Many of the victims, for various reasons, including the fear of loss of authority and dignity and of reducing their prospects of promotion, don't report such instances, and Heads too, prefer to keep them under wraps: in other words a conspiracy of silence which leads us to question the veracity of the figures published. And it is a sign of the increasing exasperation felt by teachers since no-one appears to be doing anything to really tackle the problem, that they are beginning to resort to counteraction by taking legal steps towards compensation for traumas and physical injuries sustained. In the USA one Francis Cook successfully sued a pupil for "harassment" and was awarded $35,000 damages. That won't happen here? It already has — in a High Court action against Coventry City Council in 1996 a 47-year old primary teacher, Mrs Hazel Spence-Young, received £82,500 for severe injuries (inflicted by a 10-year old) which resulted in partial paralysis of her right arm and has necessitated the wearing of a surgical collar for the rest of her life. She claimed that the pupil in question was long known to be unmanageable and should have been removed from the school earlier. "Teachers are supposed to be there to teach, not to act as riot police," she said. "When I started out on my career children were motivated and wanted to learn, but their attitude has changed."

One of the saddest and most worrying facets of the problem of indiscipline is its apparent acceptance, even on what can be an intolerable scale, by too many teachers, especially younger teachers, who were pupils themselves under an increasingly lax régime and became conditioned to regard a bit of noise and chaos as the classroom norm. This means, of course, that those of more advanced years and accustomed to a different scenario found themselves more and more out on a limb. Mercifully they are now all retired, otherwise the less compliant amongst them might have overstepped the current mark by retaliating in kind and, ironically, having themselves prosecuted for assault.

So once again we ask the question: how has this dire state of affairs ever been allowed to develop? We can blame TV films and videos and all the other awful influences to which children of uncaring parents are continually exposed, and which surely must have an influence on young, malleable minds in spite of the efforts of parties with vested interests to convince us otherwise, but the fact remains that the destructive seeds were sown in the immediate post-war years with the entrance into the educational arena of liberal-minded thinkers, chiefly educational psychologists, who were bred like rabbits and came swarming out of their incestuous burrows to tell us, as they did later when it came to the question of comprehensive schooling, that in the matter of discipline too we had been getting it all wrong since time immemorial: a silent classroom, apart from the teacher's voice and occasionally that of a reluctant pupil, made for an inhibited classroom with no outlet for self-expression; it made for a passive audience who sat there on tenterhooks and the atmosphere created lay somewhere between that of a reformatory and a graveyard. True, "spare the rod and spoil the child" was the maxim too frequently applied in those "Dark Ages" when too many strap-happy sadists used their weapon, sometimes protruding conspicuously and menacingly from a gown-pocket like a six-gun in its holster, at the slightest provocation or at no provocation at all: for hanging your coat on someone else's cloakroom peg or for a whispered request to your neighbour for a loan of his rubber — or for getting a sum wrong. In anyone's book that state of affairs should have been tolerated no more than the one which has replaced it. It has been the same old story of the pendulum which is allowed to go on swinging until it has reached the other and equally unacceptable extreme. It had reached it by the mid-70s, if not before.

But the blame for the great turnround cannot be apportioned entirely to these latter-day Quixotes. They had strong, if unwitting support, from a nascent Welfare State which rapidly spawned the notion that few restrictions should be placed on an individual's freedom and so tossed the idea of individual responsibility out of the window: citizens' rights, workers' rights (but excluding teachers' rights), working mothers (whose over-riding priority was unrestricted attendance at their place of employment and many of whom regarded schools as principally convenient dumping-grounds for their offspring) and eventually the introduction of Comprehensive Education, and the discovery that the perpetrators of anti-social behaviour either in the great outside or in schools themselves were without exception the unhappy victims of their impoverished environment. (The opponents of this facile theory had obviously not been around to witness the impoverished environments of the 20s and 30s when the people who inhabited them, old or young, still had some thought for their fellows and were grateful for any rare privileges they got). This lethal cocktail could have only one consequence, which was diminishing respect for age-old values and for those in authority, be they teachers, policemen, cinema door attendants — or their own parents, and it created a syndrome amongst the young which affected the rôle of the teacher more than that of any other because it could reduce him to a level of complete inadequacy.

So gone for ever were the days when the strength of the arm and the thickness of the Lochgelly special kept the great majority of neds in their seats and their foul mouths shut. Nowadays the only effective antidote to blatant misconduct is strength of character on the part of the teacher. But in the classroom scenario that type of strength is not altogether commonplace when you are dealing with the most incorrigible elements. In most cases it is not the fault of the teacher, for many who had no trouble at all in the 50s and 60s would have plenty of it today. The fault lies with all those who have contributed to this permissiveness and failed abysmally and unconcernedly to provide any effective alternative to corporal punishment. Taking privileges (whatever these are) away from a great hunk of a bruiser or a wee untameable firebrand are as good as useless. The greatest privilege of all is the one which neither they nor their parents appreciate — attendance at a school — and suspension from it should be the greatest privilege that can be lost. But you cannot expect such Neanderthals to think, if they ever think on such matters at all, along those lines and perhaps if parents were charged a small nominal amount for their offspring's "free" education the message might, just might, get through to them: that here is one thing that has been "free" yet must be worth having. But imagine the cries of outrage from the Lefties if such a step were ever taken. Yet many of us can remember an era when there was no charge for medical or dental care. Simple economics soon brought an end to that and maybe, by the same token, the same will happen in education. But only maybe, since people object less to paying for better health than for better schooling.

At the same time teachers themselves can be censured for putting up with the lack of support from those who caused such an eruption in the first place. A teacher, often trained largely at government expense, and therefore at public expense, should be able to walk into any classroom anywhere and conduct his lesson without interference from any quarter. Those who prevent him from doing so deserve to be branded as pariahs and treated accordingly. And — irony again — they are also the ones "given a chance" under the New Educational Jerusalem yet who spurn these same chances, while simultaneously nullifying the much better chances of others. Teachers failed themselves, when they realised that no succour was to come from any source, including their wishy-washy "unions", by not having the collective guts to demand positive action — or else — when the ominous signs of the canker first reared its ugly head and there was still time to administer an antidote.

The school situation is hardly helped by those now clamouring for a law forbidding a parent to deal an admonishing slap to his own child. Although such "reformers" appear to the normal sensible human being to be possessed by a paranoia which comes within an ace of being certifiable, their risible pleas are not always received with the contempt they deserve and it is as well to bear in mind that their like-minded predecessors are largely responsible for the present problem; and that the weirdest of the weirdies can, slowly and insidiously, get their way in the end. Consider by way of example the conclusion reached by a group of psychologists (in England) after interviewing (or should it be *counselling?*) a youngster whose main preoccupation in life was the incessant battering of his classmates: they decided that his exclusion from the classroom be terminated on the understanding that *he would not hit out more than seven times per week*. That is hailed by the zealots as a "progressive" attitude towards discipline but those of us who are still sane would no doubt have a different name for it, as we would for the intention of one authority (also in the South) to present free vouchers for food and drink to pupils who attend regularly and whose conduct is exemplary. Reminds one of a saying of Candlish's favourite author, Albert Camus: you don't shower praise on a schoolmaster because he does his job properly.

But we have no need to cross the Border to find similar examples of the potential certifiability of many of the top dogs performing on the educational stage. The Scottish Office Education Department produced, in 1977, the Pack Report on discipline and truancy and recommended that corporal punishment be phased out (contrary to the wishes of many parents and a surprisingly large number of pupils, who foresaw the likely consequences of such a radical move more clearly than its instigators). Adhering slavishly to the ideals of the recently introduced comprehensive wonderland, the Report stated that disruptive children should be integrated in the mainstream and not "marginalized in sink schools". No question of doing that, no need to do that, and "stern looks" from the teacher would be an effective alternative to the barbaric tawse. Stern looks! You would be as well trying that out on an attacking rottweiler in the final stages of rabies, and it is as bewildering as it is appalling that such a statement should be issued in all seriousness, and without fear of being held up to ridicule, by the establishment entrusted with the effective management of Scottish education. If this is the promise of things to come, as if these were not bad enough as they are, how long before pupils are granted virtually unrestricted freedom in the classroom? If the brakes are not applied firmly and soon, and the gear lever put into reverse, how long before the late 20th century's promised Utopia becomes the Dystopia of the early 21st?

It is painfully true that there is no magic wand we can wave to redress the balance. But many of us believe that society, whether society at large or within a school, has a right to be protected and that strict measures are justified if they achieve the ends which benefit the majority. What then, re-introduction of the belt or of the cane? It is interesting to note that following a TV discussion on school discipline in May 1996, 93% of the viewers who phoned in their opinion were all for the reintroduction of corporal punishment. But surely this is impracticable: the miscreants would laugh their heads off as they refused it and many teachers would refuse to administer it. And in any case the mere mention of such a monstrously regressive step, or of any other step involving coercive action, would have the publicity-seeking do-gooders foaming at the mouth and ranting on about Hitlerite tendencies. Well, reprehensible as were the methods employed by that gentleman to rid his well-disciplined Reich of all undesirable and non-contributory elements, whether they themselves were to blame or not, such a comparison would be asinine in the extreme. But we simply must throw away the powder puffs and come down much harder on the recalcitrants responsible for a classroom situation which is threatening to assume anarchic proportions. The most troublesome and persistent offenders should be roped together, literally at times if need be, in a special unit in each school where there are normally enough of them to justify its establishment, and if not in a larger area unit, with touch, thick-skinned overseers rather than teachers, whose job would be to drill their wards army-fashion with plenty of Physical Education and organized games to inculcate into them some respect both for others and for themselves. Oh, but you can't do that, the horrified will cry. And what about their right to a general education? Are they to be denied that? In fact they would not be denied anything because as unteachables their sole achievement in the classroom is to prevent teachers from teaching and the teachables from being taught. So why not give it to them in plain language which even they will understand: don't do it and you will have nothing to worry about, but cross the line and you'll be fired upon. Too simplistic? Too naïve? But is it? If it has that ring about it, then it is due to our growing reluctance as a nation to grasp the nettle when there is no other way. Omitting to provide a promising young teacher with a cogent means of self-defence against classroom turmoil is as gross a tactical error as sending the SAS into a potential holocaust with blanks in their magazines. The change-over to live ammunition is long overdue.

Candlish was one of those who strongly advocated the responsibility of parents for their children's behaviour no matter where they were, in school or anywhere else. If a teacher is still to be regarded as *in loco parentis,* as he used to be, then surely this implies that his charges have been supervised and trained in their own home and that the teacher will take over with similar authority when they are under his control. Why should he be expected to pick up the tab for the mothers and fathers who have neglected their obligations?

It has been suggested that once a pupil has accrued a certain number of "bad conduct points" his parents' family allowance should be withdrawn for a period of four weeks. In the total absence of effective sanctions and the continued presence of trendy Wendy soft attitudes to discipline, such a stratagem, especially if introduced with others mentioned, could be well worth a try. There are many adults who don't care a blazer button about the things their children get up to either in street or classroom, but touch their pockets and their beer or cigarette money and they might react differently. It's a matter of grasping that nettle again.

As for politicians, consistent in their deviousness if in little else, it appears that increasing indiscipline in state schools is something which worries them far less than the incidence of truancy: misbehaviour in the classroom, the consequences of which are unseen by, and largely unknown to, the public at large, presents less of a menace to social order than conspicuous misbehaviour outside it. Schools themselves say that parents refuse to provide absence notes or, when they do, offer the most fatuous reasons for their children's non-attendance: Primrose had to be kept at home to look after her wee brother because mother had *dyreea,* or father had to take his holidays during term-time. How else could they get a cheap package to Blackpool — or Torremolinos?

However it is hardly astonishing that members of staff, far more than the authorities would like to think, do not — how shall we put it — concern themselves unduly if habitual trouble-makers decide to take a few days off. And who can blame them? The classroom atmosphere is entirely different, the teacher is allowed to teach, pupils who want to co-operate get the chance to do so and learn a lot more than they would have done had the rabble-rousers been present. And let's forget all this claptrap about truants missing out on their education; they don't miss out on any more education when they are not there than when they are, because when they are there all they do is ensure that others miss out on theirs.

Individual schools are often criticized, by administrators who know them only by way of telephonic communication from their distant and peaceful strongholds, for their too frequent use of suspension, *** which they look upon as a sort of inverted form of truancy played by the Head and his assistants. What they really mean is: keep the beggars hidden away in the classrooms and out of the public eye. Rather should these schools be congratulated for refusing to have them on the premises.

The whole problem of escalating indiscipline is crying out for decisive and immediate action. Otherwise that nettle will fast become a cactus.

*** Exclusions of pupils from Scottish secondaries in 1992/93 numbered 25,540. This represented an increase from 1990/91 by figures varying from 137% in the Borders to 27% in Central.

Chapter 18
THE CHICKEN OR THE EGG?

We are all aware that external examinations do not furnish a complete guide to what a school may attain by way of education in the broadest sense of the term, that there can be other laudable achievements which, due to their intrinsic intangibility, are quite unassessable, but as far as caring parents are concerned performance in SCE represents the success, or failure, of their children's attendance at school over a period of 12 or 13 years and determines the vocational avenues which the nature and extent of their passes will open to them. Mum and Dad won't derive much comfort from the fact that Dougie is a leading light in the Camera Club if he managed only a D in his Higher English; or that Lorna, with her eyes set on medicine, stole the show in the end-of-term *Pirates of Penzance* if she went down in Higher Chemistry.

How large a part does an individual school play in all this? A very large part indeed, as a glance at the SCE results now published annually in the national press will immediately reveal. But is their publication necessary? Do they really tell us anything we don't know already? Not really, since top schools and attractive residential areas go together like the proverbial horse and carriage — you don't have one without t'other. If you are a childless incomer solely interested in a desirable milieu in which to live, then the figures will serve as an infallible guide. High SCE performance at Boclair Academy or Marr College will tell you that residence in Milngavie or Troon will have much to recommend it, and if you do have children you will be able to fill the bill on both counts. If on the other hand you occupy a lowly rung on the social ladder you will have little say in any case where you are housed or where your children go to school. And it comes as no great surprise that secondaries in Drumchapel or Castlemilk can claim few SCE Higher passes (in Easterhouse, an area of similar destitution, only 8% of pupils attain one or more) but a much greater number of Scotvec modules, and no need to dwell on the relative merits of each. So these so-called "league tables", if they do little else, supply, inadvertently but effectively useful information for affluent home-seekers and free advertising for up-market estate agents.

But even when group requirements have been obtained for entrance to Higher Education we find universities in particular complaining that many of their First Year students fall short of the standard they are reputed to have attained and require extra tuition to bring them up to scratch. That can mean only one thing.

Examination results can be laundered anywhere and at any time, with both ease and impunity: if you want more candidates to pass all you need do is make the questions less demanding, or the marking less stringent, or lower the passmark, or even apply all three if you wish to enhance the camouflage. It is the simplest thing in the world. When (as noted in Chapter 7) you are working with a large sample of candidates, say 10,000 in a single examination, the number who pass each year will be almost exactly the same provided the standards of difficulty and marking remain constant. If the number of passes increases substantially from one presentation to the next or over a period, say by 5% or 10%, that must indicate that at least one of the three aforementioned criteria has been applied and that consequently university and college authorities and the public at large have been deceived.

Yet politicians and examiners, when challenged over the continually increasing numbers of successful candidates, have stubbornly maintained that no such jiggery-pokery has taken place and that the improved results reflect improved methods of teaching in an improving education system. But we all know that statistics are like a bikini, concealing more than they reveal; and like other experienced teachers who had been engaged in SCE work Candlish knew — and he knew it better than most after his long and close involvement with the SCE Board as both setter and examiner — that statements of this nature were blatant untruths designed to convince all of us that everything in the educational garden was thriving and that its fecundity was fast approaching that of an Eden. He knew that pupils who had failed with a D around 1970 would have gained a C had they been born a decade later and quite possibly a B if they had sat in 1990; and it annoyed him no end that quite able children who had missed out on an essential Higher in the 1960s, and whose career prospects were thereby sorely jeopardized, would have outshone many who were passing comfortably a relatively short time later. There you have one of the vilest aspects of persistently falling standards.

    If Candlish had ever wavered in his convictions — and he hadn't — that these unwholesome practices were in operation, his experiences with private pupils in his retirement supplied further irrefutable evidence. In the main he was favoured — an hour's concentration with a backward or unwilling teenager is a trying business — in having almost exclusively smart or very smart boys and girls who needed his help only because they were being badly taught or not taught at all, nearly all of them the unfortunate victims of one or other of two imposters at Abergarvie Academy, long since welcomed aboard the comprehensive bandwagon. One of them was, incredibly, the Principal Teacher of Modern Languages, who spent most of his time in the staffroom while his class was assigned written work which was never corrected. Any teaching he did in his customary lackadaisical manner was invariably interrupted to strum a few songs on his much loved guitar. But let's be entirely truthful about this: at least they were French songs, which probably salved what conscience he had. Unbelievable? Yes, but nevertheless true. The other culprit, one of his assistants and obviously immune from any reprimand on his part, did stay with his class but for all the good he did he would have been as well keeping his Principal company during his defections. Candlish cast his mind back to his own days at Abergarvie and suspected that his old boss, Naithsmith, would be turning non-stop somersaults in the nearby cemetery. (Incidentally Naithsmith's reprobate successor was offered — and accepted — early retirement some time later and had his pension considerably enhanced. Justice would have been better done had he received none at all for he had already been swindler enough by drawing his monthly salary).

It is almost beyond belief that such fraudulent individuals can fill the position of Principal Teacher and continue to do so year after year. There aren't many of them — at least we hope not — whose utter unsuitability is so damaging to the unfortunate children for whose education they are responsible, but why on earth are they not booted out as soon as it becomes obvious that their appointment was a gross blunder? And also incomprehensible, if perhaps less manifest by virtue of their non-teaching situation, is the presence of primary and secondary Heads who are cast in the same incompetent mould; again not many, but again not a single one should exist. Some of us can recall an era when dominies and rectors were of a type admired for their scholarship and their gentlemanliness and their commanding personalities; and happily we still come across many who are endowed with these qualities, but an increasing number appear to be, in varying degrees, uninspired and uninspiring, weak and inadequate. Yet the fault is perhaps not entirely theirs: the modern concept of a school and the multifarious duties it is required to perform has made them feel like unglorified social workers and susceptible to scepticism and indifference, with their main goal their day of release. All very sad, but sadder still for being preventable.

Much as Candlish had deplored the lowering of standards in his final teaching years, he found that without a shadow of doubt these were now declining more rapidly; those who came to him for tuition, supposedly with three to five sessions of French behind them, had no more than a hazy knowledge of anything; they couldn't form the various tenses and had no idea of the function they served; in fact few of them knew what a tense was. Irregular verbs were a nightmare and they were ignorant of all but the most common words. He cast his mind back to the selective Abergarvie of the 50s and 60s, when talented pupils had covered more grammar and vocabulary by the end of their Second Year than the present generation had done by their Fifth. Even students at Sixth Year Studies level, of whom he had one or two, revealed big gaps in the basics and how they had ever got through Higher was beyond his understanding. Or was it? Because Higher French in the final quarter of the 20th Century was far removed from what it had been in the middle of it.

Candlish made no bones about the formal methods he employed. He brought his pupils up to scratch by making them learn — and *learn* in the former true sense of the term, for learning is not achieved by glancing casually at something and nothing is learned until it is *known*. If that entailed the reeling-off of strings of irregular verbs and the acquisition of vocabulary lists in their own homes, plus forms of written exercises now considered to be beyond the pale, then so be it. The wholesale condemnation of this type of mental graft, supplanted by an ultracasual approach, was the root cause of the current ills and the reason why things were not working out as they had done before. He also explained analytically French constructions that differed in conception from their English equivalents — which frequently elicited from the student the enthusiastic exclamation: "Oh, I see it now!" He was being an out-and-out reactionary according to the modern philosophy of foreign language teaching, but he didn't give a damn because it paid dividends. It was noticeable too that many of those he tutored ended up by developing a liking for a subject which they had previously detested because they had been completely lost.

At the same time Candlish did take on the occasional pupil who was quite beyond redemption. One in particular, whose parents were determined that he should be awarded Standard Grade, if only at the appropriately named Foundation Level — and what that is supposed to "found" remains obscure — nearly drove him, indeed did drive him, to distraction. Geoffrey Carson was as thick as a pikestaff, totally uncooperative, almost belligerent in his attitude. After tholing him for three or four lessons Candlish told the well-meaning father that his son didn't have the slightest hope of passing, not in a thousand years, that he was wasting his money and Candlish his time. However Mr Carson's desperate pleas finally won him over and he promised to carry on for a little longer, after which he could stand no more and sent the boy packing despite further entreaties. And lo and behold, what happened? Geoffrey was granted a C. His father was over the moon and telephoned Candlish to shower his praise on his son's life-saving tutor. Yet the life-saving tutor knew he had achieved very little because with Geoffrey very little had been achievable; the sum total of his knowledge of French could have been written on the back of a school lunch ticket, and with room to spare. If he passed, who on earth could have failed? Candlish concluded that the magnanimity of the examiners must now have reached such farcical proportions as to reduce the values of a Foundation Standard Grade, if any value it had ever had, to that of a — well, let's say a school lunch ticket.

Candlish used to ask the parents of the bright but badly taught or untaught pupils why they did not demand a hearing with the Head Teacher. This is something, strangely enough, which parents are reluctant to do; they feel they are out of their depth, not knowing quite what to say or how to say it. Apparently one or two had lodged individual complaints, but in a far less resolute manner than circumstances should have dictated, and were glibly brushed off. But the situation in the Modern Languages Department at Abergarvie

Academy had become so obviously unsatisfactory that it surely must have been, and certainly ought to have been, a subject for discussion amongst parents whose children were its casualties. If they shied away from confrontation on their own, why didn't they, Candlish suggested, present a united front? He reminded them that other considerations apart, they were paying twice for a service for which they should have been paying only once; they would be fully justified in sending his bills to the Director of Education and insisting that the authority foot them. They had every right, in fact an obligation, to create merry hell. They all agreed, but remained unwilling to accept his advice. Possibly fearing that their offspring would suffer even more by way of retaliatory measures, the last thing they wanted was to "kick up a fuss". Good God! It was due to such placatory attitudes that the endemic weaknesses of the whole system were perpetuated from one generation to the next.

* * *

It is perhaps more than mere coincidence that hand in hand with falling standards in schools and yet an increase in the number of certificates awarded that there appeared a plethora of lesser degrees and diplomas issued by new educational establishments which seemed to sprout for a spell like frenetic mushrooms, and by older institutions elevated to university status. To the ancient quartet of Scottish universities — St Andrews, Edinburgh, Glasgow and Aberdeen — were added, first of all, Stirling, Strathclyde and Heriot Watt, all of which have established themselves as reputable centres of Higher Education; then came Abertay, Glasgow Caledonian, Napier, Paisley and Robert Gordon and a number of colleges all teaching all sorts of novel subjects hitherto unimaginable. (Nor should we forget the availability of the Open University). Granted that many of the courses offered catered for the demands of modern technology (Computer Science and Genetic Engineering to name only two), but at the same time there came into being a proliferation of others which hardly seemed to come within the parameters of Higher Education as the term is generally understood: Hotel and Hospitality Management, Sports Studies, Sport and Leisure, Recreation and Leisure, Recreation Management, while James Watt College now incorporates a School of Beauty, a School of Tourism, a School of Sport and Leisure and a School of Outreach. What next? A degree in Hairdressing, in Doggie Care, in Practical Sex and Sexual Practices?

Let's look at some of the openings advertised in a single edition of *The Herald* towards the end of 1995:

Research Worker (Support Services); Research Officer (Management and Information Systems); Development Worker (Learning Difficulties); Assistant Project Leader (Day Care Services); Depute Project Leader (integration of Mental Health sufferers into community); Money Advice Worker (advice on Welfare Benefits); Assistant Assessment Officer (children with Behavioural Problems); Assistant Community Education Worker (Ethnic Minority Groups); Project Co-Ordinator (advice and assistance on Welfare Rights, Money Advice, Debts); Project Worker (young people with Special Needs). Yes, quite overwhelming, and these are merely some typical examples of the 34 vacancies appearing on the same page, with plenty of overlapping of remits to create administrative chaos and general unaccountability. And of course we must not forget the posts for Counsellors which are advertised regularly by the cartload.

And while schools were being closed (36 on Glasgow and Edinburgh's hit list alone in February 1996, which resulted in a massive protest march by parents in the capital) and experienced teachers of vital subjects retired early to save money, that did not preclude steady employment for teachers of "Personal and Social Development", "Personal Development" tutors and lecturers in "Sport and Human Body Development" or in "Leisure, Cultures and Consumption".

So an examination of the whole socio-educational spectrum unveils a myriad of intrinsically nebulous rôles for a myriad of nebulously qualified personnel. The chicken or the egg? If the chicken came first it must be beating all records for productivity.

Over the last quarter of a century our Scottish education system has become anglicized, first of all by the arrival of "O" Grade, then Standard Grade, with the final straw the proposed "Higher Still" reforms which will produce a Scottish version of a narrowly conceived English A-Level; all of these are influences which have led, and will lead further, to the kind of Higher Education and the type of indeterminate jobs outlined above.

So what does the future hold? Without a substantial input of money *in the right directions* — for a carefully conducted selection of recruits for the profession and much more effective teacher training and salaries to attract the best, without due emphasis on core subjects and on traditional methods of presenting them, and without realistic steps taken to deal with the huge problem of indiscipline, we shall continue to go on stumbling from one crisis to the next. Yet a small silver cloud is just discernible on the far horizon. After some 25 years of wanton decline it is just possible to detect signs of a fundamental rethink, of an admission in some official quarters that State Comprehensive Education in its extreme form might be injurious to the gifted and perhaps even to the more moderately endowed, that the abolition of mixed ability groups and the reintroduction of streaming might have something to recommend it. ("Diversity" and "Choice" are the latest catchwords); an admission too, if only so far in a whisper and after a precautionary glance sideways, that the much maligned "11+" or "Control Examination", despite one glaring fault, was not as evil as previously thought. Indeed John Major is even talking about having a grammar school in every town. Never too late to learn? It is unfortunately much too late for many schooled during the final decades of the 20th Century, but perhaps the first years of the 21st will bring about an improvement based on sound common sense and the experience gained from a multitude of past follies.

Note:-

The Scottish Qualifications Authority was established on April 1 1997, to take over the functions of SCOTVEC and the SCOTTISH EXAMINATION BOARD.